CW00433185

THE WITCHFINDER
GENERAL MURDERS

Jack Murray

THE WITCHFINDER GENERAL MURDERS

THE SECOND AGATHA ASTON MYSTERY

JACK MURRAY

Jack Murray

The Witchfinder General Murders

ISBN: 9798518945838
Imprint: Independently published

Jack Murray

To my Monica, Lavinia, Anne and our Angel, Baby Edward

The Witchfinder General Murders

A NOTE FROM THE AUTHOR

This is the second book in the Agatha Aston series and is very much a sequel to one of the Kit Aston series – '*The Medium Murders*'. Quite apart from recommending the series if you have not yet read it, I would direct you to this book in particular if the 'The Witchfinder General Murders' has whetted your appetite.

A warning in advance – normally I try to avoid anachronisms but clearly not having lived in the 19th century some will appear. In this book I have DELIBERATELY approached one of the characters in a particular manner that is certainly anachronistic. I would ask, however you may feel about this approach, to not give away in any future review what I've done. Treat it like you would Agatha Christie's '*The Mousetrap*'. It's a small thing but it would be greatly appreciated.

But please do consider leaving a review on Amazon. It really makes a difference...

Jack Murray

The Witchfinder General Murders

"he met with the Devil, and cheated him of his Booke, wherein were written all the Witches names in England, and if he looks on any Witch, he can tell by her countenance what she is."

Matthew Hopkins, The Discovery of Witches and Witchcraft: The Writings of the Witchfinders

"Eye of newt, and toe of frog,
Wool of bat, and tongue of dog,
Adder's fork, and blind-worm's sting,
Lizard's leg, and owlet's wing,
For a charm of powerful trouble,
Like a hell-broth boil and bubble.
Double, double toil and trouble;
Fire burn, and caldron bubble."

William Shakespeare, Macbeth

Jack Murray

Somewhere in Norfolk: 1ˢᵗ November 1876

It was a full moon.

Ignatius Pollaky looked skyward and shuddered. It was around eight o'clock in the evening. The night air stinging his face foretold a cold winter lay ahead. A light wind rustled his cloak and caused the branches of the large oak tree to creak and groan. A fluttering of feathers told Pollaky a bird had landed in the branches. He glanced up at a crow perched on the gnarled branch overhead. It jerked its head left and right. One eye studied him. Then it rasped at him as if it knew what he was about to do.

Facing Pollaky was a young woman. He looked at her and exhaled. Her hair hung down either side of her face obscuring much of it. She looked at him impassively. He'd met her for the first time less than an hour ago. They'd spoken only a few words.

Now he would kill her.

He caressed the cold metal of the revolver and wondered what age she was. Eighteen? To Pollaky she seemed older. He thought of his three girls, Minna, Rose, and Mabel. None of them were older than twelve. None of them were like this young woman. Strangely beautiful. Her eyes were clear, her skin white and the simple black dress emphasised her tall, slender frame.

The Witchfinder General Murders

The rustling of the tree was the only sound he could hear aside from his own breathing. The young woman continued to look at him. Utterly unafraid. Yes, her face and body were those of a young woman, but the eyes seemed older. Her eyes held the secrets of the ages it seemed. Knowledge passed down from generation to generation.

Enough.

He pointed the gun at her. Her eyes held his. She did not blink. He cocked the hammer. Her body was still. The oak tree swayed a little more in the breeze. Pollaky felt himself shiver.

From less than eight feet away he fired his revolver.

She collapsed to the ground. The crow flew off cawing hoarsely.

Pollaky went over to the body and looked down. He put the revolver in his pocket and bent down. Hooking his hands underneath the arms of the young woman, he dragged her a few feet towards the tree. A shallow grave had been dug. He placed the body in the grave. Lying a few feet away was the shovel he's used earlier to dig the hole. He picked it up and returned to the grave.

With great care he threw soil over the body until it was completely covered. He stood for a few minutes contemplating what he'd done. Then he walked over to the small black colt and climbed up into the saddle. He looked up. In the distance he heard the distinct sounds of hooves beating against the hard ground. A gentle kick and Pollaky's horse began to walk away.

Moments later the moon was obscured by a cloud and a darkness descended like a pall over Pollaky as he rode down the hill without looking back.

Jack Murray

1

Two Weeks Earlier...

Somewhere in Norfolk: 13th October 1876

The downpour drowned out the sound of her screams. Then the rope around her throat silenced them forever. Beneath her a dog barked an angry eulogy.

Three cloaked figures reviewed their handiwork swinging gently from a leafless oak tree. Against the night sky, the branches rose skyward, crookedly contorted, as if in pain. The tree was stood alongside a white cottage at the top of hill. Both seemed to have been abandoned by the world.

The woman was aged but not old. The hair was black save for streaks of grey running like tears down each side of her central parting. The face might have been beautiful but was now twisted in pain. Three pairs of eyes surveyed the woman. No amount of rain from the heavens could extinguish the fire in those eyes. It was the fire of obsession, fear even. Such fervour went beyond madness. It burned like ice, remote from human passions, unmoved by suffering.

Rain dripped from the tall hats of the men. They stayed still despite the rain and the wind pelting them. Soaked clothes chilled their skin, but they seemed immune. Water ran live rivulets down the back of their necks. All stood still in rapt silence as if in worship,

A crow landed on the grass underneath the woman. This made the dog stop barking for a moment. It eyed the crow suspiciously. Then the dog glanced up at the three figures in confusion. No guidance came from them on what to do, so the dog did what it always did. The barking began again, this time at the crow. From a distance. It was met with utter indifference.

The taller of the figures looked down at the crow and then glanced at the others. As if in response to the arrival of the bird, he heard a prayer being intoned. He joined in the prayer. Despite the howling noise of the rain, he heard every word being spoken. It cut through the noise of the storm, the barking of the dog, and the hoarse rattle of the crow.

The moon, which had been hiding behind dense burial-black clouds, emerged to silhouette the swinging figure in the tree. The downpour slowly transformed into a drizzle. Neither figure moved. The crow flew off leaving the dog at a loss. It stopped barking just as the prayers from the three figures ceased.

They stepped forward in unison. The younger of the men held a lamp up towards the woman. The only sound at that moment was the creaking of the tree as the figure swung backwards and forwards. They studied the woman suspended above them.

Then her eyes opened.

*

Agatha Aston sat bolt upright from the bed. She wasn't sure if she'd screamed or not. A quick glance around her bedroom confirmed it was still night. Rain battered against the windows insistently. She was bathed in sweat.

The Witchfinder General Murders

The same nightmare.

The same nightmare as the previous night. She lay back in the bed but knew sleep would not come. Frustration welled up inside her and she smacked the bed angrily. She hated missing out on her sleep.

Those eyes.

The dead woman's eyes opening. The smile on her lips before death took her, finally. There were three figures beneath the tree. One of them wore a high-crowned hat, all three sported Geneva capes and bucket-top boots. It had all been so vivid. The twisted oak by the side of the white cottage on a desolate hill.

Her mind was spinning now. Why was this dream recurring? Her first thought was that it was something that she'd read in the paper. But what? She thought about the day before when she'd been in the breakfast room reading *The Times* and The *Daily Telegra*ph. Perhaps something in those papers had attracted her attention. Or was it something she'd read absently, without really attracting her attention.

This was possible, of course. Betty had spent the morning before yesterday providing a blow-by-blow account of her latest golf round. The fact that Agatha was neither interested nor listening was a matter of little importance to her golf-fanatic friend. What was of interest and of no little amusement was the passionate frustration she was feeling with her game. In fact, her eloquence would have impressed a Billingsgate fish gutter.

It was like this with her friend. She'd known Betty Stevens since they'd met at school, fifteen years earlier. Betty was a year older, but they'd been drawn together by a mutual love of sport. Each loved to ride horses, had excelled in athletics and, with their friend Jocelyn 'Sausage' Gossage, had played in a dominant school hockey team that had been called 'The Invincibles', although rarely so outside the boundary of the school, it must be said.

Agatha lay in bed for a few minutes analysing the pros and cons of getting up. The mere act of doing this, she realised, probably was not helping her chances of falling asleep again. Then again, did she really want to sleep? It had been a horrible nightmare. All in all, it was bothersome in the extreme.

Decision made, she cast off her bedclothes and padded over to a chair where a dressing gown was draped lazily across the seat. Her slippers were under the chair. In a moment or two she was skipping down the stairs to the breakfast room. She lit a couple of gas lamps then went in search of the newspapers. All newspapers were kept in a small closet near the kitchen. No newspaper was thrown out. All were filed by title and by date. Agatha had moved into the house five years previously. They would soon need a larger space to house the collection.

Finding the newspapers from the morning before yesterday was easily accomplished. It was just after five in the morning. Flack would not be up for another two hours. There was little point in disturbing him so she made herself a cup of tea and retired to the breakfast room to scan the newspapers and search for something that may have triggered the nightmares.

Half an hour later she was asleep on the sofa, the two newspapers splayed out in front of her. She remained in this state until Betty Stevens wandered into the room and exclaimed sympathetically to her sleeping friend, 'Good Lord, woman. What on earth are you doing? Have you been drinking?'

Agatha awoke with a start. She glanced around at the newspapers in disarray and at Betty looking down at her sternly. She wondered for a brief moment if she was dreaming again.

Certainly, the face on Betty had a nightmarishly dogmatic set to it that did not bode well for whatever lame excuse that she may come up with.

Then she remembered.

'It was murder,' said Agatha, simply.

*

Betty cut a piece of bacon and handed it down to Talleyrand, Agatha's Basset who had taken up residence at her feet.

'I do wish you wouldn't do that, dear,' said Agatha. She then bent down and looked at Talleyrand in the eye. He stopped chewing the bacon and waited for his mistress to tell him off.

'You need to stop old friend. You'll never catch your lady loves if you're too chubby to match them for speed. I might add it doesn't add to your potential attractiveness either.'

Poor Talleyrand. He was perennially unlucky in love. It was his French nature. He loved ladies. Ladies loved him. Unfortunately, the ladies who loved him tended to be of a human disposition which was of little use to this Casanova among canines.

Agatha reappeared above and watched Betty polish off the last of the bacon. Let it not be said that Betty was not up to attempting two or even three things at the same time. She was reading, or rereading, the article for the umpteenth time and talking.

'It does seem a trifle lazy just to pass the death off as suicide,' agreed Betty. She fixed her eyes on Agatha. 'And you can't remember reading this story?'

Agatha shook her head in exasperation. That was the problem. She had no recollection of reading it. This would have been usual. Stories like this always piqued her interest.

'No. It's vexing to say the least. Of course, it's possible, likely even that I did. I may have been distracted.' She looked at Betty accusingly but the lady in question was mopping her plate with a piece of bread. Very continental, thought Agatha, remembering the habit Betty had picked on their trip to the south of France after Christmas last year.

'But murder?' said Betty, at length. 'Could it be because we're both at a bit of a loose end at the moment and...?' She left the sentence unfinished. They were both bored.

'The dream was very particular in that point. It was murder,' replied Agatha, tartly.

'The dream, Agatha. The dream,' said Betty waving her finger in the air perhaps in the belief that in doing so it would confirm her point.

Agatha waved her hand airily. She felt as certain as she could possibly feel that she'd had some sort of vision. It certainly felt more than just a dream. It had felt real. Almost as if she was there. This had never happened to her before. And, under any normal circumstances, she did not believe in necromancy. Yet her intuition, her instincts were telling her that the story of the suicide and her vision were one and the same. This being so, it was not a suicide, but murder.

Just one thing was bothering her, though. Each time she'd had the dream, it changed. The rain, the hanging, the dog barking, the crow flying down remained the same. Only one thing was different each time. The first time the dream had occurred she saw it from inside the cottage. She'd seen the three men hoisting the bound body upon to the tree.

In the second dream she was one of the murderers.

2

London: 18th October 1876

Blood pumped through James Simpson's body. He gulped in air like a drowning man. Ahead his quarry's long legs carrying him further away. Simpson would not have considered himself the worst athlete in the world. By anyone's reckoning he could do the one-hundred-yard-dash with the best of them. But nature had given him relatively short legs. The man he was chasing was six feet three, at least. His long stride was carrying him away.

Simpson rounded a corner just in time to see his quarry, now forty yards ahead of him, turn down another street. It was dark, the ground was slippery-cold, and Simpson would really have preferred to be in his club quaffing a few glasses of cheerfulness with Percy and the boys or with his sweetheart, Betty. Instead, he was chasing a known thief through the dark alleys of Whitechapel.

Momentum kept Simpson sprinting forward to the next alley, but he was on the point of giving up when he realised, with a feeling of exultancy, that his target had, in the dark, foggy night air of London town, inadvertently run into a dead end.

This was the good news. The bad news was that Sergeant Cartwright had long since lost touch with the two, younger and fitter men. He may as well have been back at Scotland Yard for all the use he was going to be to Simpson at that moment.

Simpson steeled himself and ran forward, turned a corner, and saw Lee 'the Lifter' Lanniston trying to scramble over a nine-foot-high wall. To give credit to his athleticism, he was perilously close to making it. But not close enough.

'C'mon, Lee, old chap, the game's up,' said Simpson.

Lee turned round to Simpson and raised his fists. His father had been a lifter just like him and his father before him. They'd never have gone quietly and nor would he.

'Gosh Lee,' said Simpson, who was bent forward, hands on knees trying to get his puff back. 'Do we have to?'

'You'll never take me alive Mr Simpson.'

These were different times, of course. Detectives could still be called Mr. Simpson. He stood up and approached Lee. He was awfully tall. Simpson also wondered if he was carrying a razor. That would put the advantage even more with him.

Lee stepped forward and his face contorted into something that he hoped was terrifying. It reminded Simpson of some poor chaps who'd had a bad tummy during the Ashanti lot. The first swing went sailing past Simpson's head by a at least a foot. The second was closer and the young detective felt the wind of it. Simpson stepped inside and delivered a short punch to the solar plexus.

Lee collapsed like he'd been hurt, which he had. He rolled over and groaned.

'What did you do that for?' asked Lee, who was clearly hurt emotionally, too.

'To be fair, Lee old chap, you did take a pop at me first. Now, up you get, it's not that bad.'

Another groan from Lee suggested that Simpson's assessment was lacking some empathy. Lee got to his feet reluctantly.

'Hand it over,' said Simpson, taking Lee by the arm and moving him into something resembling light.

'I don't have it Mr Simpson, I 'anded it over to my mate Jim Melcher.'

Simpson's heart sank. He'd missed that. Thieves like Lee 'the Lifter' Lanniston invariably worked in pairs.

Up ahead the two men saw Cartwright walking in the wrong direction. Simpson looked up at the big thief.

'Go on, Lee. Don't let me catch you doing that again.'

'Aw Mr Simpson, what can I say? You're a gent, you are. I won't do it again. I'll go straight, just you see.'

Even Simpson, a man who was trusting to a fault, hardly an ideal quality for a policeman, found this difficult to believe. Taking the unexpected gift from Simpson, gratefully, Lee spun around and jogged away leaving Simpson to face the music with his sergeant.

Now all alone on the street, Simpson hauled his tired body in the direction his sergeant had taken. A few minutes later he caught up with Cartwright who was standing outside an alehouse with a pint in his hand.

'Simpson. What news?'

'I caught him.'

'Where is he?'

'I let him off. He'd handed over the wallet to Belcher.'

Cartwright fixed his eyes on Simpson. This was never a good sign and Simpson girded himself for the inevitable carpeting.

'Did you search him?' asked Cartwright. Simpson didn't have to answer the question. He kicked himself for not thinking of this. Cartwright was shaking his head in a manner that Simpson had come to know so well. Then, from his coat pocket, he extracted a wallet. 'I came across Belcher. At least one of us had the wit to search. We can use people like him for information. Now, given you let him off so easily, please tell me you, at least, left him with the feeling that he owes you one?'

'No, sergeant,' said Simpson, morosely. 'I'll tell him next time I see him.'

'You do that, son. You do that. Now, get me another pint.'

*

The telegram had read 'most urgent'. This was something that James Simpson, now an official member of the Detective Branch since his successful trial period, had become used to with his sweetheart, Betty Stevens. Well, Agatha, if he was honest with himself. He didn't have to be a great detective to know who the instigator of the telegram was. And James Simpson was under no illusions that he was a great detective. Agatha Aston, on the other hand...

He liked Agatha. More than that, he was in awe of her. He sometimes wondered if she was a good influence on the woman, he was beginning to believe would be the one he was going to marry. Mind you, Betty gave as good as she got. He let the thought go as quickly as it had come. There was not a mean-spirited bone in Simpson's five foot eight, fourteen stone of solid muscle, body.

This made him a wonderful friend, a reliable man to work with and tremendous fun in the barrack room. It was not necessarily a qualification that would ever mark him out as the world's foremost detective. He would be better than that.

The problem was how he could broach the subject with a senior officer. He knew Chief Inspector Druscovich did not trust him since the Black-Eyed Nick affair and Sergeant Cartwright made no secret of the fact that he did not regard his abilities very highly.

Simpson sat looking at the telegram when he saw some movement in the office. He looked and it was then inspiration struck. He rose from his desk and rushed to catch up with a tall man with a bushy grey beard who was moving at a crispish pace out of the office.

'Sir,' shouted Simpson to the back of the man.

Dolly Williamson turned around reluctantly. This reluctance was partly based on the fact that he knew someone had a problem for him. It was always thus. Williamson was the Chief Superintendent, the head of the Detective Branch. The problems that reached him were never easy. He supposed this was the inevitable result of his rank. He accepted these interruptions with equanimity, but they were a trifle annoying, all the same. A second reason for his reluctance to stop was that he recognised the voice.

Dolly Williamson liked Simpson. In fact, everyone liked the young man. He was polite. Well-mannered, too. There was an easiness of manner. All in all, he was a thoroughly good egg. He was just not a natural policeman. Nature, his nature to be precise, had made him a trusting sort of chap. This was in conflict with the needs of the job which required perpetual doubt. Innate scepticism.

Williamson smiled and beckoned young Simpson over rather like a schoolmaster to a favoured pupil who had caught him two seconds before class.

'Yes Simpson?'

'Sir, there's been a suicide in Norfolk.'

'And?'

'Well sir, it may have been murder.'

A troubled look descended on Williamson that even Simpson could hardly fail to notice.

'Why do you think it may be murder, Simpson?' asked the Chief Superintendent.

Simpson was temporarily lost for what to say. Perhaps he should have been more circumspect in his choice of words. Nothing new there, he realised.

'Lady Agatha Aston, sir,' replied Simpson just in time to salvage a deteriorating situation for him.

*

'Chief Superintendent,' said Agatha, in surprise. Simpson she'd been expecting. This was certainly not what she'd anticipated.

'Betty,' said Simpson, following just behind Williamson.

'James,' said Betty with a smile. She ignored the look on Agatha's face and turned to greet Williamson.

They walked into the drawing room and sat down. Williamson disappointingly declined the invitation from Agatha to take tea. Tea normally came with a host of rather wonderful sandwiches, in Simpson's experience. It was clearly going to be strictly business.

'I understand that you believe a murder has been committed in East Anglia, Lady Agatha. May I ask why?'

Agatha, like Simpson earlier, was somewhat at a loss on how to explain why she believed a murder had taken place. To confess that she'd dreamt it would somewhat undermine the credit she'd built up following the Black-Eyed Nick case.

'I dreamt it,' said Agatha. Better to say it and face mockery than get caught out in a lie and lose trust.

'Dreamt it,' repeated Williamson trying and failing to avoid raising his eyebrows.

'I agree this may seem a little unconventional and I can readily understand that you should be sceptical, Chief Superintendent, but there you have it. I'm not a fanciful woman as, I hope, you will appreciate but I believe the suicide reported in *The Times* was murder.'

Williamson sat back and wondered if he should join Jack Whicher in retirement. His old friend and mentor had asked to be relieved of any future case responsibilities in the aftermath of the last case. A wise man thought Williamson.

'Yes, your ladyship, it is unconventional as you say but, as it happens, the local police constable in Upper Outwell happens to agree with you. I'm not sure if he dreamt it also, but there you are.'

'Are the police treating the death as suicide?' asked Agatha.

'There is a difference of opinion on the subject. The magistrate investigating the matter believes the death to be suicide. The constable and the doctor think otherwise. There will be an inquest next week sometime, I believe. It will be for the magistrate to arbitrate between the individuals concerned,' responded Williamson.

Agatha nodded and looked down at the ground. She wanted desperately to go and see for herself. She wanted to see the house in which the deceased lived; the tree from which she'd allegedly hung herself. She wanted to be asked to investigate. It was never going to happen.

'I have not been asked to send anyone,' continued Williamson. 'However, perhaps I could consent to sending young Simpson along to oversee the steps being taken to assemble evidence for the inquest. If he should happen to be accompanied by friends, then I, clearly, cannot know about this. Do I make myself clear?'

The beaming smile on the faces of the three young people in the room made it abundantly clear that they understood the Chief Superintendent perfectly.

'As it is the weekend, is there somewhere that you can stay?' asked Williamson, gazing out of the window onto Grosvenor Square, where only a few months previously the murder of Frederick Crowthorne had first brought the remarkable Lady Agatha to his attention.

'Nobby Bodkin-Brown,' said Simpson and Betty in unison. They looked at one another and smiled. It was yet further proof, to them anyway, of how Cupid's aim had been decidedly on the ball, so to speak, in putting them at the centre of a murder investigation. Together.

Williamson looked at his young subordinate and then to Agatha. He was relieved to see that she was as amusedly dismayed as he was.

'I believe the Chief Superintendent is particularly keen that we focus our energies on confirming whether or not there has been foul play.'

'Of course,' said Simpson, unconvincingly.

Betty looked a little sheepish and decided, with something approaching insight, that silence was the best policy. She reduced the beam on her face to less blinding levels.

'I trust that you can manage this situation Lady Agatha,' said Williamson.

This innocent comment might easily have been construed to mean the case however, the reply left no one in doubt as to the underlying meaning of the question.

'I shall be like an old aunt, Chief Superintendent.'

The Witchfinder General Murders

*

Williamson and Simpson parted ways outside the mansion. Simpson returned to Scotland Yard with a note for Druscovich confirming that he would spend a few days in Norfolk attending to matters related to the inquest. Meanwhile Williamson went to see Metropolitan Police Commissioner, Sir Edmund Henderson at his club. This was a weekly meeting in which he, as Chief Superintendent, updated the head of the police on all operational matters in the capital.

He liked Commissioner Henderson. Filling the shoes of a man such as Sir Richard Mayne who had held the post for thirty-nine years and overseen such change was always going to be a difficult task. In his own quiet way, Henderson had continued to revolutionise the capital's police force through both the expansion of its numbers and improving the wages of the ranks. Increasing both numbers and wages was a tribute to his adept skills at managing politicians. This skill had been notably lacking in his predecessor which meant that the job did not exactly attract the brightest individuals in upgrading the professionalism of the police, Henderson was perhaps the first Commissioner to make the connection between police funding, votes and political ambition.

After running through the usual agenda with Henderson they arrived at the last item. The face of Williamson darkened.

'Regarding Meiklejohn and Clarke I have not received any response to my letter. I fear the worst Commissioner.'

'Meaning?'

'Meaning that I do not know how deep the corruption goes,' explained Williamson.

'Druscovich?'

Williamson nodded, sadly.

19

'Clarke?'

Another nod from Williamson.

'Is there anyone you can trust?'

'Littlechild,' replied Williamson.

The meeting ended on this point and Williamson declined Henderson's offer to stay on for lunch. As he was leaving Henderson touched his arm. Williamson turned around in surprise.

'There was one other item I wanted to mention.'

'Yes, sir?' asked Williamson, putting on his coat.

'I had my attention drawn to an apparent suicide of a woman in Norfolk.'

Williamson's mouth fell open. This was the third time he'd heard about the death in as many hours.

'I gather it's a suicide. But we should send someone along anyway just to keep an eye on things. Strange place. They do things a bit differently out there if memory serves.'

'Coincidentally, I've asked for someone to go there only this morning, Commissioner.'

'Oh, jolly good. Not someone too senior, I hope. We don't want to scare the horses,' said Henderson with a smile.

'No, he's new. Not even a sergeant.'

'Good. As I say, don't want to create a stir.'

Williamson thought of Lady Agatha. His acquaintance with this young lady had been brief but he had little doubt that she could create a special kind of mayhem in the right situation. This was not what troubled him at this moment.

'How did this come to your attention, if I may ask, sir?'

He looked hard at the Commissioner, but Henderson's face betrayed nothing except an irritation at the inconvenience of it all.

'Duff,' replied Henderson. 'He's the local Member of Parliament. He sent me a telegram.'

Williamson nodded then said, 'May I see the telegram?'

This surprised Henderson and his sense of irritation increased.

'Why? What on earth's going on?'

Williamson explained wearily, 'I have heard about this case, sir. I gather all may not be as it seems.'

'Meaning?'

'It could be murder, sir,' said Williamson and he meant it.

3

Holbrigg Hall, Norfolk: 20th October 1876

The trip to Holbrigg Hall took the three companions a day to complete. An early morning train from Liverpool Street Station conveyed them to Norwich. From Norwich they hired a private coach to transport them to the Hall which was located near Fakenham in the north of the county.

'I say,' said Betty, who normally did, 'We could go for a swim. Do you swim James?'

'Like a fish,' said Simpson as jovially as the prospect of swimming in the North Sea in the mouth of winter could inspire. This horrifying prospect was poo-pooed immediately by Agatha, much to Simpson's relief.

'Nonsense dear. You'll catch hypothermia.'

Simpson had not yet reached that elevated position for a man in a relationship with a. woman where he could utter even a syllable in contradiction. Most men in love rarely attain such a level of expertise in their ongoing commerce with the assertive sex. The expert practitioner not only can avoid opinions, but he can also make it seem as if it was his beloved's view all along. Perhaps only Percy Baines amongst Simpson's friends had attained such pre-eminence. Of course, he was an out and out cad. Sound chap, though.

The Witchfinder General Murders

'I didn't bring a swimming costume,' said Betty sadly, looking directly at her sweetheart. The eyes of the young man widened just enough for Betty to feel her bosom swell in happiness at the delightfully wicked thoughts she had deliberately engineered in the young man's mind. Simpson was no amateur in these games, however. His response was quick.

'Nor I, sadly.'

Such repartee invariably provoked strong reactions in Agatha. Thankfully, Agatha's mind was oblivious to the, frankly, wanton exchange between the two would-be lovers. Her gaze was fixed out the window, her mind turning over what she could remember about the dream.

There had been no dream the previous night. Thankfully she had taken the precaution of writing all that she could remember. Frustratingly, the gap between vividness of the dream and what Agatha could recall was enormous. Staring out of the window had done little to sharpen her recollection.

The journey from Norwich took almost as long as the train journey and the skies were beginning to darken as the Hall came into view. Despite the gloom, the Hall was a spectacular sight. Holbrigg Hall was a wonderful example of English Palladian style. Built one hundred years previously using local yellow brick, surrounded by acres of rolling parkland and a beautifully blue boating lake, the Hall was a testimony to a period of English architecture that was in thrall to classical Rome.

'Very Whiggish,' was Agatha's first comment upon seeing the wonderful exterior.

Simpson nodded in agreement without any earthly idea as to what Agatha was talking about. He had taken to doing this of late for the understandable reason that Agatha, if not always right, was certainly better informed than he. The ticklish problem that she might ask why he agreed had, thankfully, not occurred. According to Betty, Agatha was unlikely to probe further. She neglected to add that this was because she was uninterested in other people's opinions, anyway.

The carriage pulled up at the entrance. Waiting to greet the party was Norbert 'Nobby' Bodkin-Brown, the youngest ever holder of the title, the Earl of Manningfield. Nobby was built to a similar design specification as his friend and former comrade-in-arms, Simpson. Of average height, above average girth, and below average intelligence, Nobby was as optimistic and jovial a chum as any chap could wish to have.

'Simps,' exclaimed Nobby by way of greeting.

'Nobby, dear chap,' replied Simpson.

'Betty,' exclaimed Nobby, who, it appeared to Agatha, spoke in exclamations.

'Nobby,' said Betty in a tone of voice that was exclamatory, too.

'How's that shiftless brother of yours, Rory?'

'Shiftless as ever,' confirmed Betty, laughing.

'Hello Nobby,' said Agatha offering her cheek.

'Agatha, my dear, a pleasure as always,' said Nobby in a voice that was distinctly calmer but no less warm.

Nobby invited the party inside and soon all were shown to their rooms. A shadow of disappointment fell over Betty's face when she realised that Agatha's room lay directly between hers and Simpson's. Not that she would have done anything but, still, it was the *idea* rather than the act, wasn't it?

As it was near dinner time, the ladies elected to remain in their rooms to make ready. Simpson joined Nobby in the billiards room for an aperitif. Nobby played the first shot.

The Witchfinder General Murders

'So, what's all this about then?'

'There was an apparent suicide just outside a village near Fakenham, Upper Outwell,' explained Simpson.

'I say. Are you suggesting that there may have been foul play?'

'Quite possibly. The attending constable had his doubts about the affair.'

'Really? Do you know why?'

'I'll find out tomorrow. I will be going to the village to meet him tomorrow along with the ladies.'

'The ladies? I say, Simps. Is it not a trifle strong? I mean, I know Agatha's a terribly clever girl but still...'

'You've hit the nail on its bonce, old boy. There's certainly a lot going on upstairs with Agatha all right.'

The two men laughed conspiratorially.

'I quite like what's downstairs, too, if you take my meaning. Of course, I'm happily married now, but still, one can view the pictures in the gallery without owning them, so to speak.'

'Where is Olivia, anyway?'

'She's with her coven over in Holt,' replied Nobby making a face and twisting his hands into claws. 'She'll fly in on her broom later.'

The two men laughed, and the game continued for another half hour before they, too, retired to dress for dinner.

Notwithstanding the shorter amount of time each man had dedicated to their dressing for dinner, both appeared, almost miraculously, before the ladies. Nobby's opportunity to pontificate on why this should so be cut short by the arrival of Agatha and then Betty. Both looked fetching in, recently acquired, dark gowns. The men nobly commented on the beauty of their companions. Compliments duly despatched and received meant that everyone could relax and enjoy the evening ahead.

They were joined a few minutes before eight by two other couples. Doctor Laurence Wilson and his wife Cynthia were in their fifties, but their evident good humour and ease of manner made them appear younger. The next guests were only a little older than Agatha and Betty. Joseph Parr, and his wife Amy were as darkly attractive as they were severe of countenance. He was a lawyer. An ambitious one according to Nobby, with an eye on going to London and becoming a Queen's Council. He was the youngest son of the Earl of Thetcham, whose estate occupied a few thousand acres to the east of the county.

'Olivia will be here presently,' announced Nobby. 'She's back from Holt and is just getting ready.'

Ten minutes later, Countess Olivia swept into the room using the more traditional method of walking rather than the broomstick her husband had suggested earlier. She was carrying her black cat, Jinx. Born Olivia Amethyst, she was as tall as her husband with long raven-black hair and green eyes. She was also one of the most beautiful women Agatha had ever seen. Sadly, her beauty was matched by an arrogant streak that made her annoying company. Agatha had disliked her since their first meeting at Nobby's wedding three years previously. She doubted time or rank would have softened the edges of a distinctly prickly personality.

The men stood up to greet her whilst the women remained seated. A swift glance at the other ladies in the room suggested to Agatha that they were no more enamoured with the Countess than she was. Agatha was curious enough to wonder why and woman enough to be wholly delighted by this observation.

The Witchfinder General Murders

Nobby and Olivia made for a very contrasting couple. At first glance one would have been forgiven for thinking that she had merely married the cheery former army officer, now Earl, for his title. In this, first appearances aren't always deceptive. Agatha knew little of Olivia's past, but she was not known to come from a good family and there was something of the actress about her. As a rule, Agatha tended to care little for knowing about the background of men or women who married her friends but perhaps Olivia might make an entertaining exception.

'I'm so sorry,' declaimed Olivia, sounding anything but. 'I hope you'll forgive my being late.'

'Nonsense, dear, you were just in time to make your usual grand last-to-arrive entrance,' said Nobby with a lot less hostility than the jibe suggested.

Olivia looked at her husband and laughed. It seemed genuine to Agatha. Like a private joke that they both enjoyed. Perhaps there was some hope.

Olivia sat down and Jinx immediately took up residence on her lap.

'Did I see a Basset hound when I arrived?' asked Olivia generally to the table.

'Yes, that's Talleyrand,' said Agatha. 'I do hope your cat won't bully him. He has a dose of the morbs at the moment, poor thing.'

'Oh, I'm terribly sorry to hear that,' said Olivia. 'Why, may I ask?'

'He's formed an attachment with a poodle a few doors down from our house. His feelings are unrequited, alas. I think he's missing her. He hardly raised a growl all the way here.'

'Poor thing. Perhaps we can introduce him to some of our dogs,' replied Nobby, 'Lord knows we've had quite a few.'

The food was soon served, and it was excellent if the relish with which Betty and Simpson attacked it was anything to go by. One of the things that Agatha and Betty liked about their friend Nobby was that he made no distinction between men and women in the conversation at the table. Anything from hunting, horses, and puppies through to politics was considered fair game.

'I see the Americans have made rather a hash of their general election,' said Dr Wilson. What do you make of it Parr?'

Parr dabbed his chin. It looked like he was preparing for eighteen holes thought Betty with a sinking heart.

'I agree, it's an extraordinary situation when someone can win the popular vote but potentially lose the election because of their electoral college. Coming just after our election two years ago when exactly the same thing happened. I've been arguing for years that we need to redraw our boundaries to provide a fair apportionment of the votes.'

'I'm sure you have, dear,' said Olivia quickly. It was clear she'd recognised the same danger signs as Betty and was swift to act lest the young lawyer detail exactly what he'd been saying. 'Has anyone read the first part of the latest Trollope? I think Plantagenet Palliser would make a wonderful Prime Minister; don't you think?'

The discussion moved onto the merits of the fictional Palliser versus the two giants of British politics, Disraeli, and Gladstone. The discussion over dinner was noteworthy, in Agatha's view, for one thing. No one asked why she and her friends had come to visit. This might have been deemed

28

impolite but there were ways of broaching the subject that could allow for the guests to expand on their plans over the next few days.

While this did not trouble Agatha, she was curious to see what reactions the subject might prompt. She looked for an opportunity to mention it as the discussion on the aftermath of the Battle of the Little Big Horn drew to a close.

'May we borrow some horses, Nobby, tomorrow?' asked Agatha, as dessert was served.

'Blancmange, excellent,' said Simpson who'd said little during the political discussions.

Nobby confirmed there were many horses they could choose from but refrained from asking why or where.

'We'd like to visit Upper Outwell. It's only a few miles from here I believe,' explained Agatha.

There was a moment's hesitation before Nobby smiled almost in relief and confirmed that three horses would be made ready for them. Parr was surprised, however.

'It's less than half an hour away. Have you friends there?'

Agatha turned to Simpson at this point. Alas, Simpson was demolishing the blancmange with a gusto that suggested a request for a second helping was but moments away.

'James has been asked by the head of the Detective Branch to look in on an inquest taking place there. A suicide.'

Parr and Wilson both spoke at the same moment. The doctor quick ceded the field to the young lawyer.

'As it happens, I am going there myself tomorrow. Perhaps I can come with you?'

'Are you involved in the inquest?' asked Agatha.

'I was asked by the local magistrate, Colonel Magilton to help. Of course, I said yes.'

Agatha smiled and nodded to Parr. Then she turned to the doctor and said, 'I believe Dr Wilson, you were about to say something.'

'The local doctor attending this matter is our son, Frank. But are you sure about going Lady Agatha? It's rather a tragic story and I'm not sure what possible interest it could hold for you.'

Agatha gave Simpson a gentle kick under the table. It really was time for him to stop scoffing for a moment. Thankfully, Simpson had woken up to the ongoing discussion.

'Lady Agatha and Lady Betty were requested specially by the Chief Superintendent to join me.'

Agatha would certainly have choked on the Blancmange at such an outrageous lie had she not already passed hers to Simpson. The lie gave truth to the idea that sometimes in life, if one must descend to an untruth for the greater good, don't stint. Think big. Make the falsehood so colossally unlikely that it gives the sceptic pause for thought lest they appear to be small-minded or simply ill-informed.

Agatha and Betty held their collective breaths as the fib detonated in the minds of the dinner guests like a belch at a burial. It was Olivia who spoke first.

'Well, I for one, am delighted, that women can be seen as something other than vehicles of procreation or cooks.'

'I quite agree,' said Nobby more dutifully than passionately. He smiled at his wife. The love light was strong as far as Agatha could see. And why not? Whatever one might have thought of her personality, it was Agatha's experience that men were remarkably forgiving when the lady in question was as spectacularly attractive as this. Agatha was undecided on whether this was a recommendation for men or confirmation of their lack of common sense.

'Well, I hope you won't find the matter too disturbing, Lady Agatha, Lady Elizabeth,' said Wilson. 'Of course, it was probably a suicide which is tragic enough. I just hope they find her daughter.'

Agatha and Betty exchanged glances.

'Daughter, you say?' responded Betty.

'Yes. The dead woman's daughter has been missing since the suicide.'

*

'Did you sense a marked reluctance to discuss our reasons for coming?' asked Agatha when dinner had ended, and everyone had retired to their rooms.

'No, I didn't notice anything. You did?' asked Betty.

'I would hardly have remarked on it if I hadn't,' pointed out Agatha, primly. Betty rolled her eyes and ignored her friend. 'I'm not quite sure if I like the idea of this lawyer accompanying us. I had the sense that he wants to superintend our activities.'

Betty disagreed with this and felt Agatha was being overly suspicious. The subject of Olivia was met with greater concurrence.

'Well, I'm not sure whether to congratulate Nobby for eschewing rank or condemn him for choosing the beautifully insubstantial over someone of greater depth,' said Agatha.

'She is rather striking,' agreed Betty. She thought of Simpson. He was not anyone's idea of a Greek god, but he was handsome after a fashion, well-made and a gentleman all the way from his head to his toes. And likeable. 'If I were a man, I can see why she would have tempted him. I think he adores her. And I think she genuinely loves him.'

Agatha looked at Betty in surprise. These were her thoughts also, but she was curious as to why Betty should say so.

'It's a feeling, dear. I can't say there's much by way of science or evidence to support the hypothesis. Anyway, I'm curious to meet Dr Wilson's son, tomorrow. I wonder what he's like.'

The Witchfinder General Murders

4

Holbrigg Hall, Norfolk: 21ˢᵗ October 1876

Joseph Parr joined Simpson and the ladies soon after breakfast. He was riding an impressive chestnut colt. Agatha and Betty were immediately smitten by his mount. Nobby provided them with two silver mares and Simpson was given Nobby's own horse, a black pony with a white stripe on its nose.

They rode across fields and only occasionally took the road. Betty stayed alongside Simpson who demonstrated no little skill in handling a rather spirited horse. Agatha rode ahead with Parr. This had been agreed the previous night. Any hopes that Parr would enlighten them on the case, however, proved fruitless as the lawyer admitted he'd not yet been involved. Agatha took this to mean he was well informed on the case but had no wish to share what he knew. Once more, it seemed, there was a marked reluctance to discuss the matter with outsiders. Agatha had little doubt the reason was not solely related to her sex.

'It's no more than twenty minutes,' said Parr as they set off. This was said in the manner of a pronouncement rather than general conversation. Betty found this aspect of Parr somewhat irritating, but Agatha seemed to take a certain amount of sport from asking the lawyer his opinion on all manner of subjects. Parr was just the man to give it.

Beliefs and judgements issued forth from the young lawyer with the volume and velocity of a river approaching a waterfall. Agatha felt that he was providing her with an education. Had the journey lasted much longer she would almost certainly have come away from it much improved. She said as much to Parr who bowed nobly little realising the extent of the mockery to which he was being subjected.

Betty and Simpson joined them later in the ride. The two men discussed in detail, prompted by Agatha, the merits of coarse versus fly fishing. This brought a frown from Betty who could tell by the light in Agatha's eyes what her friend was up to.

They trotted through all manner of country. Nearing the village, they passed through a wood, black and silent. Hanging branches of willow blocked their path like crooked arms and gnarled fingers trying to ensnare an unsuspecting traveller. The ground was freezing hard, glistening with frost. On one side they saw a lake, coal-black and threatening. All were wrapped up well against the cold, but Agatha could feel its sting on her cheeks. She welcomed it. Horse riding was one of the joys of her life and it always invigorated her. The only drawback was they were not travelling more quickly.

Parr, at least, proved accurate in his assessment of the journey's length. They reached the village of Upper Outwell just over twenty minutes after setting out. The village was slightly larger than Agatha had been anticipating. There was one main street which led to a large square with a green in the middle. Directly in front of it was a church made from Norfolk Carrstone. Beside the church was a church hall made from timber. On the other side of the square was an inn and a village store. Dotted around the street and further back were one storey cottages. The population would certainly have been in the hundreds rather than the tens.

On the green a number of labourers were laying out planks of wood. There was also a frame being constructed in the centre of the green by two men and one woman. Agatha was impressed to see the woman, hammer in hand, placing a nail on the wood and gently battering the life out of it.

The party went to the local inn, 'The Pheasant', named after that noble bird which spends the greater part of its short life in Norfolk getting blown out of the sky by sportsmen.

Constable Tibbins and the son of Dr and Mrs Wilson, Frank, were waiting for them. If this were a novel from one of the lesser genres, such as romance, then Dr Frank Wilson might have been accurately described as tall, dark, and handsome. One might even have thrown 'brooding' into the mix, were one so inclined. In the pages of more high-minded tomes related, for example, to crime, then Wilson seemed to be strikingly intelligent with dark, mysterious eyes.

Wilson turned his attention to Simpson, first, after the initial introductions from Parr, clearly requiring an explanation from the man as to why women were also attending the inquest. This, of course, was obviously because he was a policeman rather than any doubts over the capability of the ladies to explain their own presence. Simpson did the honours in explaining why Agatha and Betty were there.

'Lady Agatha and Lady Elizabeth are working with the Metropolitan Police in a private capacity. It comes from the top.'

The latter part of the sentence was said out of earshot of the ladies. Tibbins scratched his head. This was a reflex action when he didn't understand something. He scratched his head a lot. What became apparent very quickly was that the mild-mannered constable had no idea if the death of Mrs Carr was suicide or not. He'd been guided in this opinion, somewhat, by the young doctor.

'We'll meet Colonel Magilton, the magistrate, at the cottage where the Carrs lived,' said Wilson.

'Is it far from here?' asked Simpson.

'Only a few minutes ride.'

Tibbins looked at Wilson and scratched his head, again. He clearly did not have a horse.

'We'll see you in an hour, constable,' said Wilson striding towards the door.

The gentlemen followed the ladies out to the horses. Agatha sensed Dr Wilson catch her up.

'Lady Agatha, I hope you'll forgive my reaction to you and the presence of your friend. I wasn't expecting...'

'Women to be working or women to be working with the police?'

The doctor laughed easily. It was a pleasant sound and there was no attempt on the part of Wilson to dissemble.

'I could say the latter, Lady Agatha, but we both know I'd be guilty of mendacity.'

'Then I shall forgive your lapse if you tell me why you think that Mrs Carr was murdered.'

This stopped the young doctor in his tracks. Agatha stopped, too. They regarded one another for a moment then the doctor smiled.

'May I ask why you say this?'

'I have no idea if it's true or not. But I am utterly certain that Constable Tibbins has no idea what happened, which means that it is either you or the magistrate who believes this poor woman was murdered. I've decided it's you but I'm willing to admit this is based not on evidence but...'

'Intuition?' said the doctor, smiling.

'Yes. I often think that intuition is an instinct abused by women and underused by men.'

The doctor gave Agatha a hand up onto her horse and then mounted his own in one swift movement. Betty, meanwhile, caught the eye of her friend. It would be fair to say that one eyebrow was raised. She was met with the ghost of a grin.

They set off at a brisk trot. Leaving the village Agatha noticed two older women stop and look at them. Perhaps it was her imagination, but she sensed that both women knew who they were and why they were in the village. They made no attempt to avert their eyes from Agatha.

The party rode up a hill and over its crest. Ahead was a small wood which they skirted around. Once they were past the wood, the cottage came into view. Betty turned to Agatha to ask her if it resembled what she'd seen in her dream. The question froze on her lips. Agatha's face had become distinctly paler. For the first time in as long as she could remember, Agatha seemed afraid.

'From the dream?' asked Betty at last.

Agatha nodded.

*

The cottage was white, single storey with a high thatched roof. To the side was a well with an old, rusted bucket. On the other side of the house was an oak tree which had split sometime in the last century. Its branches twisted at grotesque angles high into the sky. Tied near the tree was a horse which Agatha guessed belonged to the magistrate.

Jack Murray

As Agatha dismounted, she gave a barely perceptible nod to her two friends. This was the signal that the cottage was identical to what she'd seen in her dream. The doctor was, once more, in attendance to help Agatha from the horse. Although she, under any other circumstances, would not have needed the help, she felt a little reckless. What harm would it do? His hands grasped her waist, and she enjoyed the feeling of being lifted down.

'Colonel Magilton is awaiting us I see,' said Wilson. He did not seem particularly happy about this, further confirming Agatha's suspicion that it was Wilson who believed that foul play had taken place. He glanced at Agatha and noticed how she was walking and twirling around at the same time.

'Are you well Lady Agatha?' asked the doctor.

Agatha glanced at him archly and replied, 'Do you wish to examine me?'

'Do you wish to be examined?' replied Wilson in an instant. There was a very attractive smile lurking behind his eyes that both recognised. It was very apparent that the doctor was enjoying the game of cat and mouse as much as Agatha.

'Perhaps it's a little public here,' suggested Agatha, fixing her gaze on the doctor. He smiled and they walked to the door. They reached it just behind their three companions.

Colonel Cedric Magilton was a large man from whatever starting point you wished to choose. He was taller than the tall doctor with a wide frame and plenty of meat to the bone, rather like that recent introduction to the fields in the area, the Norfolk Red Poll cow.

He was also Northern Irish. From Antrim, he explained when he saw the reaction of the visitors to his accent.

'I've been in England forty years now. My friends back home think I've become too English.'

The Witchfinder General Murders

'They can't be referring to your accent, sir,' laughed Betty. 'It's beautiful. I could listen to you all day.'

A glance from Wilson to Agatha suggested that if they stayed long enough Betty's wish might be granted. The big Ulsterman professed himself delighted to meet Simpson and the ladies. To his credit he showed no surprise that the ladies should even be there. Instead, he offered a view of labour relations that bordered on Chartism.

'I'm delighted the Metropolitan Police wishes to employ women. More women should be given an opportunity to work in professions associated with men. Makes eminent sense to me.'

'What is your view, Dr Wilson, on such heresy?' asked Agatha when Magilton had finished.

'I will bow to Colonel Magilton's greater experience and wisdom,' said Wilson which neither satisfied Agatha nor seemed convincing to the speaker. The doctor sensed his answer had been disappointing when Agatha turned away from him in a manner that suggested a chill had descended on the room.

Simpson then asked the colonel which regiment he had served in. This led to a brief conversation where the two former army men shared their regiment details. Magilton had been a Colonel in the artillery and served in India and East Africa. Agatha smiled throughout the exchange in a patiently impatient manner. She was keen to get on with the business in hand. A glance to Betty was met with a nod: message received.

Betty communicated to her beloved in a manner that women have used for centuries. She fixed her gaze on Simpson and raise both eyebrows. Simpson understood immediately and ceased forthwith to encourage the loquacious Ulsterman from indulging his visitors with too many stories from his time serving Queen and country.

'Can you tell us, sir,' asked Parr, 'What transpired two nights ago?'

'Of course, Mr Parr. Perhaps I can have one more attempt at persuading my young friend to the rational view. Well, as you can see, we are in the cottage of Mrs Ophelia Carr. She was a widow. Forty years old.'

'When did she lose her husband?' asked Agatha.

'I believe it was some four years ago. She came to live here soon after.'

Agatha looked surprised at this. She asked another question, 'She was not from this area?'

'She was. The house belonged to her mother. The lady in question passed away two years ago from natural causes. She'd been ill for some time, I gather. Mrs Carr and her daughter returned four years ago, as I was saying.'

Magilton paused for a moment and smiled benignly at Agatha.

'I can see a question forming on your lips already Lady Agatha. Where is the young lady and why, if she has disappeared, do we believe we are dealing with suicide?'

Agatha nodded. So did Simpson who had now caught up. His notebook was out, and pencil was at the ready.

'Perhaps Dr Wilson can take over at this point and speak of the daughter, Evelyn. Doctor?'

Wilson nodded to Magilton and then addressed the visitors.

'Evelyn Carr is eighteen years of age and, sadly, a much-troubled young lady. On two occasions that I know of, she tried to run away from home.'

Once more Agatha interjected.

'Was there a romance involved?'

The doctor shook his head. He seemed rather sad.

'Quite the opposite. Miss Carr is an attractive young woman and would surely have had many potential suitors from the village had she so chosen. Her manner, though, was difficult. She had no friends that we know of. As I was saying, she was a very troubled young woman. I would hasten to add, Lady Agatha, that her choice not to have any sweethearts is not why I say she was unhappy.'

Agatha smiled and acknowledged the doctor's perspicacity. The good doctor, meanwhile, sensed he'd regained some credit in the eyes of this extraordinarily assertive young woman. A short silence followed then the doctor continued.

'Miss Carr suffers from a condition that I have labelled dysphoria.'

Agatha frowned for a moment. The replied, 'As opposed to euphoria.'

'Precisely, Lady Agatha. Evelyn was not suffering from any form of delirium or melancholia. Far from it. She was in all respects a very balanced young lady. She had higher spirits and greater energy than someone suffering from melancholia.'

'How did this manifest itself, doctor?' asked Betty, who was listening as intently as Agatha.

'Evelyn was, for want of a better description, always restless. In a state of permanent dissatisfaction that seemed greater than what one would normally associate with someone young. It felt as if she was trying to break out from something.'

'Like a butterfly from the chrysalis?' asked Agatha, who was clearly intrigued.

'That is very apt, Lady Agatha.'

Simpson came forward with a question of his own, 'Is there any possibility that this is a case of matricide.'

Agatha turned sharply to Simpson. She'd been wondering the same. The surprise was that Betty's sweetheart was familiar with the term never mind on the same track.

Wilson shook his head.

'I have been attending the young lady for two years now. I cannot reconcile the Evelyn I knew with that of a cold-blooded murderess. It's inconceivable. I would add it would also have been quite a feat for a slip of a girl to lift Mrs Carr and hang her. Just the physical effort to disable her mother and then hoist her up on the oak tree would be beyond her. No, I believe that only two possibilities exist. She committed suicide as Colonel Magilton believes or she was murdered. By a man, I should add.'

'Or men,' added Agatha. Wilson looked at her sharply.

'Or men,' he agreed.

'What evidence is there for saying she was murdered?' asked Betty.

Wilson glanced at Magilton before replying.

'Two reasons, Lady Elizabeth. Firstly, the fact that Evelyn is missing suggests to me that she has either gone into hiding or has been taken by the same people who murdered her mother.'

Agatha had been pondering just the same point. Was Evelyn in hiding or had she been kidnapped?

'The second reason is, and I can scarcely believe that I am saying this, there is Mrs Carr herself.'

Magilton shuffled his feet and everyone turned to him.

'Really Wilson, is this necessary. We cannot use hearsay as a potential motive for such a serious crime.'

The Witchfinder General Murders

Agatha looked at Wilson with an arched eyebrow that suggested he should get on with it.

'It is widely believed,' said the reluctant Wilson, 'that Mrs Carr was a witch.'

5

There were several seconds of silence. Shocked silence.

'I say,' said Simpson and Betty in unison. Agatha rolled her eyes. This was becoming more than an irritation. Simpson put into words what the visitors were thinking.

'She was murdered because she was a witch?'

Wilson could not reply and merely nodded, his face reddening. Magilton, meanwhile, beamed benignly at the visitors in the manner of a man who senses he has been proven right but has too much by way of good manners to say so when a self-satisfied smile could do the job more annoyingly. Agatha found him immensely irritating.

'Norfolk is certainly famous for having had witches in the past. Wasn't the Witchfinder General, Matthew Hopkins from this part of the world?' asked Agatha.

'That is so, Lady Agatha,' replied Wilson, looking gratefully towards her.

'Come now, Wilson,' said Magilton, still smiling despite his obvious irritation that the view had not yet been dismissed out of hand, 'we are in the nineteenth century. We are in the midst of such progress in technology and science. Can we really talk of witches?'

'Whether or not I personally believe in witchcraft is hardly the issue, Colonel Magilton. You would concede that many people still do. That being the case, is it not beyond the realms of possibility that Mrs Carr suffered because of this perception? You are from the area, sir, you know the rumours as well as I.'

'Not quite from the area, sir, but I have become aware of the rumours. But just as I can disregard idle gossip from the illiterate, I can equally dismiss the likelihood that Mrs Carr, who has lived in the area these past four years, suddenly became hunted like a witch from two hundred years ago. Surely, Wilson, you can see that this makes no sense whatsoever. And what about the suicide note?'

For the second time in the space of a few minutes the room fell silent and all eyes turned to Wilson. Even Agatha, whose sympathies for the doctor had waxed and waned like sunshine on a cloudy day, found herself frustrated by the way material evidence like this had not been dealt with up front.

'Suicide note?' said Agatha, glaring at Wilson.

'We do not know if it was a suicide note,' said Wilson, grimly. 'As the colonel well knows, portions of the note were burned.'

'How do you mean?' asked Agatha.

'What Dr Wilson is saying is that the note was retrieved from the fireplace. It seems Mrs Carr wrote the note and then decided to throw it away. It was partially burned but enough remained to indicate her intentions. She was quite clearly contemplating taking her own life.'

'Why would she do so if she had a young daughter?' pressed Agatha. This seemed to her inconceivable.

'Not so young, Lady Agatha. A young woman. Not just a young woman, someone who wanted to be away from her mother. She had not been seen for at least three days prior to the death of her mother. The note makes it plain that Mrs Carr felt she would never see her daughter again and she took her own life.'

Agatha could hear Wilson behind her breathe out noisily which suggested complete disagreement. Not just disagreement, frustration, too. Wilson had no evidence that Magilton was incorrect in his assessment. Yet, Agatha believed Wilson. She was reluctant to admit in this public forum that this was due to a dream. She felt a stab of guilt at this, but nothing would be gained by saying something like this. It would only undermine belief that women were capable of being involved in such weighty matters.

She sensed Wilson's eyes were on her. Turning around she looked at him whilst shaking her head imperceptibly. Wilson nodded in response. He understood that this was not the time to speak about the dream.

For the next ten minutes Agatha, Betty and Simpson contented themselves with finding out more about what had led to the discovery of the body and subsequent events.

The body had been found by a friend of Mrs Carr, Miss Beatrix Dahlia. She was a regular visitor to the cottage and had found the dead body around eight o'clock two mornings previously. She had immediately alerted Constable Tibbins and the doctor. A funeral was planned for the next day with Reverend Martin Lumley presiding. Letters had been sent out to police throughout the county containing a description of Evelyn Carr, but they had yet to receive a response.

For the last ten minutes the party were given a tour around the cottage and then the grounds outside. There was no evidence to suggest that Mrs Carr was a witch. A point made by Betty in her usual fashion.

The Witchfinder General Murders

'I don't see any books of spells or grimoires. Rather disappointing. Mind you, that broom looks sturdy enough to support someone.' Betty picked up the broom and through a leg over it and said, 'What do you think?'

Simpson and Magilton both roared with laughter, but Agatha noticed that the young doctor was not amused. This was interesting. A medical man. A man of science who appeared, at least to Agatha, to give more than a semblance of credence to the stories regarding the dead woman.

Agatha felt disheartened. Barring any new evidence, she suspected that the colonel, as acting magistrate, would find that the death was caused by suicide. This would immediately end any investigation. Would that be such a bad thing, however? This could always be overturned later on. The advantage of such a finding was now apparent to Agatha. She and Betty would be given a free hand to continue their inquiries without any interference from the police. The more she thought about it the more the idea appealed.

Nobby would have no problem with Agatha and Betty staying a little longer. One other thought also struck Agatha, but she dispelled it as soon as she could. It would mean more time with Dr Wilson. Unfortunately, at twenty-five, such thoughts were difficult to rid oneself of. They hung in the air like the sweet smell of flowers in spring.

And were just as welcome.

*

The ride back would have been a silent affair had Agatha had her way. Unfortunately, Parr, who had remained quite silent during their meeting with Magilton, suddenly became quite vocal in support of the suicide theory.

'It's clear that the poor woman had lost her mind and committed suicide.'

'Women do not have the same mental strength as men,' agreed Agatha in a tone of voice that immediately had Betty's senses on alert. Agatha in sporting mood was always good fun as long as you were not the object of the sport.

'Sadly, this is true Lady Agatha but, if I may say, it does you credit that you should acknowledge this. If I may also say, you represent an exception to what is a general rule.'

'Thank you, Mr Parr. I fear that I am probably prone to all of the same weaknesses, fancies, and prejudices of my sex.

'You are too modest Lady Agatha.'

And you are too stupid for words, thought Agatha.

It is a natural law of nature that the more someone advocates a position on which you have a more neutral opinion the stronger your opposition will become. It's almost Newtonian. The more Parr spoke, the more he convinced his travelling companions that further investigation was necessary.

As they rode back into Upper Outwell, they saw a lot of activity taking place on the village green. The frame in the centre of the green was higher now. The planks of wood were being turned into various stalls and bunting lay between each stall. It looked for all the worked like a village fete. Given the time of year, this was unusual.

Agatha turned to Wilson for an explanation. The doctor smiled and said, 'The village makes a great deal of celebrating Hallowe'en. Perhaps more than most. Probably a remnant of the county's association with witchcraft. It's a pity that you will not be around next week to see it.' Something in the doctor's smile suggested that his interest was more than just showing a

visitor a local village tradition. Whether it was related to her or
to the case remained a subject of conjecture.

Agatha smiled back at the doctor, 'I should love to see the
Hallowe'en festival. Perhaps we will come back. What will be
burned?'

'Satan. Well, it's meant to be Satan, but it hardly looks like
anything, really.'

'I wonder what the local vicar thinks of this,' said Agatha
wryly.

'He's quite broad-minded. I sometimes wonder if he actually
believes in God.'

Agatha erupted into laughter. She loved indiscreet talk. The
more indiscreet the better. The others looked at her, but
Agatha was not going to let on what had amused her so.

'Perhaps tomorrow, Lady Agatha,' said Wilson in a low
voice, 'You can tell me more about this dream.'

Agatha looked at the doctor archly and replied, 'And you
can tell me how long you've felt it appropriate to eavesdrop on
conversation between women.' Agatha had guessed he had
overheard the conversation with Betty.

'I only do it when the women interest me, Lady Agatha.'

They arrived at 'The Pheasant' just as the doctor said this.

'Will you stay for lunch?' asked Wilson.

Agatha declined on behalf of herself and the others
explaining that they wanted to return to their friend, the Earl of
Manningfield. Parr elected to stay in the village claiming that he
had some business to attend to there.

'Do you know the way back?' asked Parr.

'I think we can manage,' smiled Simpson, who was a lot less
put out by the patronising air of Parr than his two companions.

The two men doffed their hats and watched the party set off in the direction from which they'd come.

'I think they know more than they profess to,' said Parr as the group crested the hill.

'I agree,' said Wilson.

*

'I think that Colonel Magilton has no intention other than to find for suicide,' said Betty as the group left the village.

Agatha's attention was momentarily diverted by seeing the two women she'd seen earlier standing at the doorway of a house on the edge of the village.

'Yes,' agreed Simpson. 'The only problem is that if he does so then I shall have to return to London. There's not a shred of evidence to suggest she was murdered, and we have the suicide note.'

'Which we have not yet seen,' pointed out Agatha. 'Magilton will have to produce it at the inquest on Monday. Also, let's come back next week for Hallowe'en. It looks rather fun. I'm sure Nobby will want to come too.'

'Will the doctor be there?' asked Betty, eyeing her friend closely.

Agatha smiled and replied, 'He suggested it.'

'Perhaps we should just accuse him of murder now and have done with it,' laughed Betty.

Agatha laughed at this but winced a little, too.

'It would be just my luck,' she smiled.

'Well best that we establish his innocence before you go falling for any killer,' advised Betty.

'I admit nothing,' responded Agatha but the grin on her face suggested even she was not convinced by her answer. Simpson, meanwhile, was oblivious to the conversation happening and studying the cows with great interest.

'These Norfolk Red Polls really are quite the thing now. Look at the withers on them.'

Betty didn't dare look at Agatha, but she did hold a finger up to warn her about saying anything to her sweetheart.

'Spoil sport,' said Agatha by way of retort.

They followed the same route that Parr had taken earlier that morning. The rain held off and the crisp October air was a blissful change from the stench of London. Without weekends in the country, Agatha felt she'd go mad.

This was not just in a different county but another world. The smells and the colours were beautiful rather than repellent. London might have been the epicentre of progress in the known world yet here, barely a few hours away, it seemed they were in a different century.

They arrived back at the estate just before one o'clock in the afternoon. After handing over the horses to the stable boys, the three friends went to the house to dress quickly for lunch.

'Where's Talleyrand?' asked Agatha to the butler, Kent.

'He spent most of the morning in the yard, my lady. I believe he's sleeping now, in the library.'

'I see,' said Agatha and turned to go upstairs. As she started climbing a thought occurred to her.

'I say, Kent.'

'Yes, your ladyship.'

'Were there many other dogs in the yard?'

'Oh yes, your ladyship. Talleyrand appeared to be having a most enjoyable time playing with them.'

'I see,' said Agatha. A thought occurred to her, but she dismissed it quickly and skipped up the stairs to wash and dress.

Jack Murray

6

After a ploughman's lunch, Nobby suggested they spend the afternoon down at the lake on the boats. As there was little more, they could do on the case that day everyone agreed readily. Agatha wandered over to look for Talleyrand. She found him still dozing contentedly in the library.

'Hello old fellow,' said Agatha. She began to stroke him behind the ear. 'Do you fancy joining us for a little sail on the lake?'

Talleyrand opened one bleary eye at Agatha and mumbled an apology if Agatha's intuition was correct. The effort of keeping this eye open proved too much and he resumed his slumbering state.

'Well, whatever you were up to this morning certainly tired you out,' said Agatha rising from her seat and going off in search of the others. She found them in the entrance hall.

'Forward march,' said Nobby. They headed outside. It was overcast but otherwise dry.

As they marched down to the lake, Olivia took Agatha's arm and insisted on hearing everything that they'd learned regarding the death of Mrs Carr.

Agatha told her all of the facts of the case without proffering an opinion on what she'd heard. Thankfully, Olivia was considerably less restrained in this respect.

'I can't abide Colonel Magilton. If ever a man seemed more pleased with himself with scant reason to be it is the good colonel.'

Agatha could not help but laugh which Olivia took to be agreement. With good reason, too. Olivia, oddly, seemed to be much more companiable than she'd remembered. Perhaps she'd misjudged her. Sometimes she was too quick to assess people. It served well, most of the time. Not always, though.

'I suspect that it will take a confession from a murderer before our colonel admits there's any possibility of foul play,' continued Olivia.

Agatha shot Olivia a look, but the wife of her friend chattered on happily.

'And there's no word of where Evelyn might be?'

'No,' replied Agatha, carefully. 'That remains a mystery.'

'Yet the colonel sees no reason to question the disappearance. I find this extraordinary, Agatha. The man is an imbecile.'

Agatha would have not gone quite so far but it was always entertaining to hear the upper classes in full vitriolic flow against their vassals. They arrived at the lake and separated into two boats. Nobby and Olivia took Agatha in one dinghy whilst Betty and Simpson were given time to themselves in another dinghy.

The dinghies set off with Nobby manning the oars in one and Betty manning them in the other. Simpson, meanwhile, lay back with his hands behind his head and enjoyed the ride.

'She seems rather smitten with him,' said Olivia knowingly to Agatha.

Agatha looked at the other dinghy and would have been far pushed to disagree.

'Can we expect wedding bells soon?'

'I don't know about soon,' admitted Agatha. There seemed little question that it was now only a matter of time. Simpson and Betty had spent as much time as they could together since the Black-Eyed Nick case. Simpson had taken up golf, a game he'd played occasionally, with an enthusiasm that matched that of Betty. It was a tribute to the game that its refusal to give up its secrets easily intensified the passion that Simpson developed in their early outings. Like a cat, golf is not a game that is easily mastered or brought to heel.

'I hope so,' continued Agatha. 'I rather like him.'

'Simps is the best,' agreed Nobby. 'No finer chap. Why I remember one time...'

Nobby stopped at that point as he remembered the punchline of the story involved stripping some new member of their club, painting his bottom black and leaving him in the middle of Blackheath with no money.

The two ladies looked at him expectantly. It must be said neither doubted for a second that the story might have been of more robust nature than was usually considered appropriate in mixed company. The dawning realisation on Nobby's face was exquisite. Olivia was not a woman to let him away with this. A fact that made her go up, once more, in Agatha's estimation.

'Go on Nobby my dear, tell us more. I'm sure Agatha is as desperate to hear the story as I am.'

'Uhm, well my dear, perhaps another time. I seem to remember it was not quite as funny as I first thought.'

The two ladies looked at him as sternly as two ladies who are highly amused at a man's discomfort normally do. Nobby reddened and increased the pace of his stroke claiming that they could get near the swans and see the signets.

'I see the village is preparing for the festival,' said Agatha changing the subject. 'I should love to see it. Do you go, normally?'

'Oh yes,' said Nobby. 'Every year.'

This seemed to earn him a rebuke from Olivia although nothing was said.

'You're more than welcome to stay until next week,' said Olivia.

'Well, I do have to return to London after Monday's inquest but perhaps we might come down next weekend. The festival is Tuesday week. Would you mind?'

'Of course not,' said Nobby. He seemed quite enthused by the idea. It was harder to tell if Olivia was as happy with the idea. Agatha sensed that she was studying her. It was difficult to know what to make of this. In fact, Olivia was definitely proving to be a different proposition to what Agatha had thought her since she and Betty had attended the wedding three years previously.

'Do you normally attend church on Sunday mornings?' asked Agatha. She was curious to meet the Reverend Lumley.

'Yes,' replied Olivia, 'You can join us in the carriage. We'll leave around nine thirty. The service is at ten. I'll introduce you to Reverend Lumley if you like.'

Agatha glanced at Olivia. There was something indefinable in the look. Unexpected too. Agatha felt unaccountably ill at ease.

*

Agatha and Betty were the first up the next morning. As was their habit, they devoured the Sunday newspapers with as much relish as their breakfast. Since the Black-Eyed Nick case, this included the *News of the World.*

The Witchfinder General Murders

'Anything new from that awful man Rampling?' asked Agatha.

Robbie Rampling had been at the forefront of breaking stories on their previous case thanks to his collaboration with the private inquiry agent, Ignatius Pollaky.

'Nothing of interest,' replied Betty. 'Just tittle tattle.'

Betty knew this would be sufficient to pique her friend's interest. Agatha duly put her Telegraph down and looked eagerly at her friend.

'Dame Margaret Hopwood's husband runs off with maid,' announced Betty with some glee. 'Do you remember we saw her last year in Macbeth?'

'Hideous performance.'

'She should have played one of the witches; all that screaming,' said Betty.

'I've seen mannequins that were less wooden.'

'Speaking of screaming women, I thought I heard some screams last night,' said Betty.

Agatha looked up from the newspaper in surprise.

'Really? When was this?'

'Soon after we retired. I couldn't sleep and went for a walk at the front of the house,' explained Betty.

'Where were they coming from?' asked Agatha, intrigued.

'At a guess I would say from the floor above ours. At the front of the house.'

Agatha did a mental calculation of the architecture of the house. Then a slow smile crept over her face.

'Were these screams or would you say more like a moaning sound?'

'Actually, it was more like a moaning sound. You don't think the house is haunted, do you?'

Agatha reassured her friend that the house was unlikely to be haunted. She didn't add that if it were then it was probably the ghost of Casanova visiting Olivia in the middle of the night. There was, perhaps, a more corporeal explanation instead.

The two ladies were finishing breakfast just as Simpson and, a rather fatigued looking, Nobby made it to the starting gate.

'Off already?' asked Nobby.

'Taking Talleyrand for a walk. He needs the exercise,' replied Agatha.

'The old chap was fairly well exercised yesterday,' replied Nobby with what could only be described as a chortle. At least that was Agatha's interpretation. Quite what it meant was open to conjecture, but some suspicions were forming in Agatha's mind.

Talleyrand had enjoyed several strips of bacon and seemed a new dog from the rather bushed Basset he'd been not a day previously. There was distinct spring in his step, an alertness of eye and his tail was up.

'Looks like the sleep yesterday did him good,' suggested Betty.

Agatha studied the hound and frowned a little. Talleyrand looked up expectantly at Agatha as she put the leash on. They stepped outside the front door.

'Looks like rain,' said Betty who was protected against the elements by her usual Harris tweed jacket, skirt, and cap. They went down to the lake and used the time, away from the house, to chat about their impressions of the last two days.

'It's an odd place,' suggested Betty. 'Perhaps I've become too accustomed to London.'

'I agree,' replied Agatha. 'It's not altogether unpleasant but I can't quite grasp what it is that makes me think you're right. Everyone is friendly but...'

'It does feel as if they're holding something back.'

'Exactly. I feel uneasy for some reason.'

As to what that something was neither could guess. Rather than speculating further the conversation veered towards the happier subject of James Simpson.

'Olivia was asking me about how serious things are between you and James.'

'What did you say?' asked Betty laughing.

'I told the truth. I wasn't sure. It's only been a couple of months.'

'True, and he hasn't broken one hundred yet over eighteen holes.'

'He'd better up his game, then,' laughed Agatha.

'I said as much to him. I mean does he expect a woman like me to commit myself to a man that can't make it, at the very least, into the nineties. It's unthinkable.'

'Quite right, too,' agreed Agatha. 'What happens if he becomes better than you, though, dear?'

'Then I will have met my lord and master,' responded Betty erupting into laughter.

Agatha, too, was giggling uncontrollably, particularly when her friend added, 'I do think it's a sign of the progress when courtship involving clubs is confined to hitting small white balls rather than women over the bean and carrying them off to a cave.'

*

The carriage set off a little late necessitating that they hurtle along the road at a clip that had the passengers falling into each other's arms at frequent intervals. Nobby, as good-hearted as he was, could not prevent himself from looking accusingly at his wife whose lateness had caused the need to rush. Olivia, recognising that it was her tardiness that had caused them to be riding at such a dangerous lick had the decency to apologise.

'I'm so sorry,' said Olivia arranging her hair as she'd, once more, fallen to her side.

It seemed only Betty and Simpson were not in the least minded by the discomfort of the journey. Collapsing into Simpson's strong arms was as pleasant a way as any to spend a Sunday morning. After the second tight corner had been negotiated, Agatha found herself averting her eyes. It appeared that Simpson was interpreting his responsibilities in protecting his sweetheart rather too liberally if where his hands were gripping was any guide. Certainly, Betty seemed grateful for his aid.

As the service couldn't begin until the squire took his seat, Reverend Lumley waited by the window in the rectory for the arrival of Nobby. He rolled his eyes when he saw the carriage pull up at St Evanora's with a minute to spare.

Nobby hurried with Olivia and their three guests down the aisle seats set aside for them at the front. Agatha nodded to Dr Wilson who was sitting on one side of the aisle. They took their seats as Mr Trimble, the organist, began to play the opening hymn. Reverend Lumley appeared as if on cue and led the singing of *How Firm a Foundation.*

The Reverend Lumley was around sixty years of age with ruddy cheeks, bushy whiskers and a mild-mannered smile that did not leave his lips throughout the service. It seemed nothing could be more delightful to him than to be with his flock on a Sunday morning.

The Witchfinder General Murders

Lumley's sermon was notably devoid of fire and brimstone but a gently amusing reflection on the fragility of life. He referred to the sad passing of Mrs Carr but did so in a way that was as compassionate as it was enlightened. Nothing in his comments suggested he thought her death anything other than the last act of a woman who had lost the will to live. There was no condemnation of her action just a wish for the repose of her soul.

The service lasted just over an hour and a half. Agatha could sense Betty's impatience with the continuous singing. Not one but two hymns signalled the end of the service. Thankfully the noise of the organ and the singing drowned out the sound of her friend's disapproval.

It was drizzling gently outside as Olivia fulfilled her promise to introduce Agatha and her companions to the Reverend Lumley. Up close he was tall, lean and every bit as welcoming as he'd appeared on the altar.

After the opening pleasantries Lumley asked Agatha and Betty how long they intended staying.

'We leave after the inquest, tomorrow,' explained Agatha.

'Inquest?' replied Lumley in surprise. He looked at the two ladies again with undisguised alarm at the prospect of their hearing the unseemly details attending to the death of Mrs Carr.

Simpson explained, not for the first time, why the ladies were accompanying him. He did not elaborate on the nature of his friendship with one of the ladies in question.

'Well,' chuckled Lumley after hearing Simpson speak, 'It's a long time since I was last in London. I can see things are changing there.'

'So, they should,' said Agatha with twinkling eyes.

'Quite,' replied Lumley which was hardly a ringing recommendation for the progress of women in society.

The arrival of Dr Wilson denied the ladies the opportunity hear any other syllables from the reverend on this or any other topic.

'Lady Agatha,' murmured Wilson. 'We can't keep you away from our little village.'

Agatha fixed him a smile and replied, 'I'm sure Colonel Magilton is poised to deliver a verdict that will surely see our departure.'

'I fear you may be right,' replied Wilson. The Reverend Lumley, meanwhile, moved off in search of less challenging members of the congregation leaving Wilson temporarily alone with Agatha. The doctor smiled at Agatha and said, 'May I show you around?'

'Nothing would delight me more Dr Wilson,' said Agatha giving him her arm.

7

He walked with her towards the green. Work had been suspended as it was the Lord's day. Wilson acted as Agatha's guide. He pointed out the stalls. The first one, explained Wilson, would be a Punch and Judy show. Another would be stocks for the children to throw cream pies at the unfortunate prisoner and then there was the wood frame being erected in the centre.

'This is a bonfire,' explained Wilson.

'I hope it doesn't rain. This might dampen the festivities, somewhat,' suggested Agatha.

'I have been attending this festival on and off for over twenty years. I cannot remember one occasion where we have experienced even so much as a drizzle.' Wilson held his hands out and looked heavenwards as he said this.

'Remarkable. It seems you have divine providence to thank.'

'Or spells,' chuckled Wilson.

Agatha shot him a glance, but Wilson seemed genuinely to be joking so she smiled, too. A thought struck Agatha as she studied the frame.

'Why do they burn Satan? I've never really associated him with Hallowe'en'.

'Nor I, I must admit,' smiled Wilson. 'There's no written history of the village. It's been around since the Saxon times.

However, it changed from being an encampment to something a bit larger, according to folklore anyway, with the arrival of Nathaniel Goodfellow some eight hundred years ago. For as long as anyone can remember, the village celebrates its founding by burning an effigy of Satan. This always takes place the night before All Hallows Day.'

Agatha nodded her head and grinned, 'I love the very pagan Christianity of it.'

Wilson laughed, 'I like that description. Do you mind if I steal it?'

'Be my guest, Dr Wilson. Do you make a habit of stealing things normally,' asked Agatha, staring deep into the dark eyes of the doctor. It was a challenge of sorts. Would the doctor pick up the gauntlet, wondered Agatha?

'Hearts, Lady Agatha, only hearts.'

'I don't know why, Dr Wilson, but I think I believe you.'

Across the green Agatha spied the two older women she'd seen the previous day. They had walked over to a young man who was sitting on the wet ground. The young man was rocking back and forth.

'That's Ned,' said Wilson. His voice bled with sadness. 'He's...' Wilson paused for a moment as he sought the words that would describe the youth.

Agatha put her hand on his.

'I think I understand. Poor thing.'

She looked at the two women crouch down and give him something to eat. The empty eyes of Ned showed no gratitude. He took the bread and ate it without hunger or pleasure. When he'd finished, he stared straight ahead at the half-built wooden frame. Agatha felt a sadness for the youth. Had he parents?

What would become of him, if not? Did the village look after him or ignore him?

Agatha became aware, again, that the two women were looking at her. She felt as if she should go over and speak to them but what would she say? A slight pressure on her elbow told her that Wilson was wishing to lead her back towards the church. Agatha turned around and saw Betty with Simpson chatting to Reverend Lumley. Nearby, Nobby was with Olivia near the carriage. It looked as if everyone was waiting for Agatha to return.

'I think I shall deliver you unto your friends,' said Wilson.

They walked over to join the others by the carriage. The rain was beginning to fall more heavily now so little needed to be said to persuade everyone that it was time to go.

'Adieu, Lady Agatha,' said Wilson, touching his hat.

'Until tomorrow, Dr Wilson.'

Wilson helped her into the carriage and Agatha took her seat beside Olivia who smiled conspiratorially at her.

'He's rather good-looking wouldn't you say?'

Agatha laughed but made no response. To confirm this would merely have been to state the obvious whilst, at the same time, leaving one open to all manner of speculation from a lady who probably lived and breathed such tittle tattle.

Within minutes they were heading out of the village. Agatha found her eyes returning once more to the poor youth who sat alone rocking backwards and forwards, ignoring the pleas of the two ladies to come inside.

*

'He seems to like your library,' said Agatha gazing at the napping Basset. 'Well, I'll take the advice of the ages and let him lie.'

Betty had gone for a hike with Simpson which could have meant any number of things at this stage in their friendship. At twenty-five, Agatha did not feel she was up to the role of chaperoning her friend every hour of the day and was happy to leave the two sweethearts to the rolling hills, the countryside, and the rain.

As she was in the library and the day looked less than enticing, Agatha decided to investigate the extensive book collection. It was impressively serious. Leather bound first editions of French and German writers were heavily in evidence as well as a good selection of Ancient Greek and Roman texts, translated. Agatha's heart sank. There was little that she could get her teeth into there. The appeal of melancholic French and German writers had long since waned although she retained a soft spot for the Brothers Grimm. Perhaps Nobby had a private collection of penny dreadfuls somewhere.

She strolled past a small collection of medical and scientific tomes. She'd read Newton's *In Principia* at school. Once was enough. A couple of black leather books caught her eye and she wandered over towards them. If their covers looked interesting, then that was as nothing to the title and the content.

The first book was quite slim. It was titled '*The Discovery of Witches*'. She looked inside. The name of the author was familiar: Matthew Hopkins. The first page read: Delivered to the Judges of Assize for the County of NORFOLK. And now published by MATTHEW HOPKINS, Witch-finder, for the benefit of the whole KINGDOME.

A charming man, no doubt, thought Agatha in disgust. The idea of a man being paid by the state to murder women on the flimsiest of evidence appalled her. Yet it had been a relatively widespread practice at one time and particularly so in Norfolk.

66

The Witchfinder General Murders

She wondered for a moment what the basis for the convictions had been. Jealousy, vengeance and lies would unquestionably have played their usual sinister parts. Fundamentally it was about hatred and fear. Hatred and fear of women to be precise.

As frustrating as she found the restrictions placed on women in the latter eighteen seventies, it represented extraordinary progress from the life her sex had endured only two centuries previously. Yet it wasn't enough. Until women could not only vote but stand alongside men in Parliament; until they could work alongside men in offices, factories, farms and in government; until they could have control of their own income rather than have it handed over to their husbands then women would never truly be free citizens in the United Kingdom. She closed the book by Hopkins. She felt sullied by touching it.

She turned her attention to the second book: the *'Pseudomonarchia Daemonum'*, which appeared to be a list of demons and *The Magus* by Francis Barrett, a grimoire which collected together magical rituals. There were a number of books on Astrology. Ebenezer Sibly's *'A New and Complete Illustration of the Celestial Science of Astrology'* caught her eye and she glanced through it briefly.

While she had an innate scepticism of witchcraft, she also felt an admiration for this band of women. They had been respected by large portions of the community in which they lived. Women and men came to them. They had something which the men valued beyond what they traditionally required from the sex.

She leafed through the book. Unfortunately, it was written in the impenetrable English she'd so detested since when she'd been forced to read Chaucer at school.

Agatha passed an hour in the library before spying her friend and Simpson strolling hand in hand towards the mansion. That part of the estate was open to the elements and they were battling against a wind blowing a light drizzle into their faces.

Both were soaked to the skin and happily oblivious to their state. There was no question her friend was as happy as she could remember, and Betty had a naturally optimistic outlook on life. Perhaps the time was coming soon when she'd leave the house on Grosvenor Square. This created a conflict in Agatha that she refused to acknowledge but could not entirely dispel either.

Her reverie was interrupted by the snoring of Talleyrand. The Basset had been inexplicably contradictory. He seemed to veer between extremes of puppyish energy and elderly fatigue. Perhaps the country air was tiring him out. Or something else.

The door to the library opened a few minutes later and Betty entered, sodden. She took off her cap but lacked a small statue to test her 'throw-the-horseshoe' skill on. She settled for stuffing it in her pocket.

'Are those the witchcraft books?' asked Betty, catching Agatha by surprise.

'Good Lord, how did you know?'

Betty walked over to Agatha's seat and looked at the books arrayed on the table. 'I was here before dinner and had a look around. Don't think much of their books. All a bit...'

'Serious?'

'Dull.'

'Has James any thoughts on tomorrow?'

'He agrees with us. The inquest is a foregone conclusion. The colonel is going to confirm that it was suicide and that will mean James' involvement will end until any new evidence is brought forward.'

'And Evelyn Carr?'

'Aside from circulating her name and description to police forces around the country, he cannot pursue the matter any further. He's not senior enough yet to dictate these matters.'

Agatha nodded absently. There was no use in feeling frustrated towards Simpson. He would be handed a new case to work on. However, Agatha was under no such command structure. She fully intended keeping the matter alive. She glanced up from her seat.

'What's that in your hair?'

Betty extracted some straw that caught itself in her bun at the back.

'Good Lord. However, did that get there?'

Agatha studied her closely and said wryly, 'How indeed.'

Betty reddened somewhat and walked over to the sleeping Talleyrand.

'Still sleeping old fellow?'

'Must be something in the air,' replied Agatha sardonically. She already had her suspicions related to her hound's contrasting moods at different times in the day. It seemed as if he was not alone in this regard if the straw was anything to go by.

As she said this another thought struck her. It was something she would need to follow up as soon as she arrived back in London. She smiled at the idea. It was almost too funny.

She told Betty her idea. Betty nodded thoughtfully and then said, 'Wonders, truly never cease.'

8

The inquest began at nine o'clock with the entrance of Colonel Magilton accompanied by Parr to 'The Pheasant'. Agatha, Betty, and Simpson had been joined by Olivia, who was curious to see the proceedings. Nobby declined stating that he'd rather be shooting pheasant than stuck in the inn of the same name listening to Colonel Magilton, whom he could not abide.

Agatha looked around the room. Magilton and Parr were sitting at the top of the room at tables laid out horizontally in the long room. Beside them was a clerk who was tasked with writing down the proceedings.

A number of villagers were attending including one of the older women Agatha had noticed on her previous visits to Upper Outwell. She sat at the back. Dr Wilson was sitting at the front alongside Constable Tibbins. Agatha guessed that they would be the principal witnesses in the inquest. In this she was not quite right. There was one other. After calling the inquest open, Magilton called the first witness. It was Beatrix Dahlia.

Beatrix Dahlia stepped forward and sat just opposite the Magilton. The colonel smiled benignly at the lady and confirmed her name and her address.

The Witchfinder General Murders

'Please Miss Dahlia, can you tell us what happened on the morning you found Mrs Carr.'

In a clear, if rather tremulous voice, Beatrix Dahlia recounted what had happened that morning. Agatha put this down to nervousness at having to speak in front of an audience or perhaps it was emotion. She was clearly well educated. Her voice gradually lost its tremor as she spoke.

'I often called on Ophelia. We have, had, been friends since first she arrived in the village. I arrived at the house just after eight. That's when I saw her.'

Miss Dahlia broke down and wept for a few moments as Magilton urged her to take her time in a voice that suggested he wanted her to hurry up. Whether it was the kind consideration of Magilton or a desire to finish her testimony, Miss Dahlia picked up where she left off.

'I went immediately to look for Evelyn, but she was not there. Ophelia hadn't seen her since the day before yesterday.'

Magilton asked the clerk to make a note of the date that Evelyn had last been reported seen by her mother. Then he asked Miss Dahlia, 'Has Miss Evelyn often spent time away from her mother's cottage?'

There was a slight pause before she responded, 'Yes. On two or three previous occasions she had spent a night sometimes two away.'

'But she always returned home?'

'Always.'

'Do you know where she went? Did she ever say?'

'No,' answered Miss Dahl immediately. Agatha felt the response was almost too quick. It brooked no follow up from Magilton which, Agatha suspected, was her intention. She doubted, though, that Magilton would be taken in by this. The colonel seemed to accept the fact that Miss Dahl would not be more forthcoming on this subject, so he took a different tack.

'Is it your belief that Evelyn was present when her mother lost her life?'

'I cannot say, sir,' replied Miss Dahlia. The answer did not impress Magilton but as he had no further questions, he thanked her and allowed her to leave the makeshift witness stand after she confirmed that her next action had been to locate the police constable.

The next witness was Constable Tibbins. The constable was, if anything, even more nervous than Miss Dahlia. As his testimony progressed, unimpeded by questions from Magilton, Agatha wondered if it was because he was trying to appease two masters.

'Miss Dahlia came to my house around eight thirty and alerted me to the tragedy. I knew that we would have to remove the body of Miss Carr, so I called on John Lodge and told him of what had happened. Then I called on Dr Wilson. The three of us arrived at the cottage around fifteen minutes later.'

'What did you do then?'

'Dr Wilson established that Mrs Carr was dead and then the three of us took her down from the tree and placed her in a cart. Then, accompanied by Dr Wilson, I made a search of the cottage for clues as to what might have happened.'

'What did you find?' asked Magilton.

'Our first thought was to locate Miss Carr but there was no sign of her in the cottage. Then we looked on the table and drawers for anything that might have given us an indication of her state of mind. Then we found the suicide note.'

'Who found the suicide note?' There was something approaching a smile on Magilton's face as he asked this.

'Dr Wilson found the note in the fireplace.'

'Was the note burnt?'

'Partially sir but we could still read what it said.'

Magilton then held up a small piece of paper to the gathering.

'I have here the piece of paper that was found in the fireplace.'

This caused a murmuring amongst the people who had crowded into the inn. Magilton reached over and handed the paper to Constable Tibbins.

'Will you read for us the note, Constable Tibbins?'

Tibbins seemed to freeze in the spotlight of attention. For an awful moment Magilton heart stopped also as the, very real, thought occurred to him that Tibbins might not be able to read. However, Tibbins fished into his pocket and extracted a pair of spectacles. He put them on and began to read.

'The opening part of the note was burned so half of the opening three lines are missing. It reads: "for the best. I cannot....there is no future for me. I do this knowing I shall find a peace that I could never have had on this earth." It is signed Ophelia Carr.'

Magilton leaned forward, once more there was a gleam of triumph in his eyes when he asked, 'Constable Tibbins, can we be certain that this note was written by the hand of Mrs Carr?'

'Yes sir. We found other items which contained her signature.'

Magilton held up a clutch of papers to the court like a priest holding a host to his congregation.

'In my hand I have the papers referred to by Constable Tibbins. We will return to these later. Thank you for your testimony, Constable Tibbins. I would like to call the next witness. Dr Francis Wilson.'

Wilson was sitting beside Tibbins so did not have to move from his seat. The colonel asked Wilson to recount his memory of what had happened on the fateful morning. His testimony was identical to the policeman's. Magilton asked if Wilson had any knowledge of the whereabouts of Evelyn Carr. Something in the manner of his asking struck Agatha as odd. She leaned forward.

Wilson replied, 'I have no idea where Miss Carr has gone.'

Magilton seemed not hear him correctly for he fixed Wilson a look that might have resembled a lion contemplating its next meal.

'No idea whatsoever?' asked Magilton. This seemed to Agatha an extraordinary question to ask. Certainly, the features of Wilson turned from stone to outright dislike.

'None, sir.'

Agatha sat back in her seat. What could have prompted such an exchange? Agatha sat back and pondered for a moment and then it struck her.

Were Dr Wilson and Evelyn Carr sweethearts?

This would certainly account for the inference implicit in the question and its follow up. Quite what this meant for the case, Agatha was unsure but with each passing second the atmosphere in the inquest grew more tense.

'You have examined the letter signed by Mrs Carr. Do you believe it was her hand?'

Wilson, at last had a chance to offer an opinion rather than solely recount the events of the morning or reveal something that he either did not know or wished to hide.

'I am a doctor not a handwriting expert. I cannot say if this is the hand of Mrs Carr or, indeed, if it is a suicide note. The note proves nothing in my eyes. Instead, it potentially begs more questions.'

Magilton had clearly expected this answer and his response was measured.

'Would you acknowledge that there are strong similarities between the writing on this letter and the writing in the papers I showed earlier.'

'Yes, but that does not mean...'

'Your answer is yes, then,' said Magilton coldly. This was said in a score-settling tone of voice. The two men glared at one another. No attempt was made to disguise their mutual antipathy.

The question remained unanswered and Magilton decided not to press the point further. Instead, he moved onto another area.

'You examined the body of the deceased. Can you tell us the cause of death?'

'The cause of death was a broken neck caused by hanging. I estimate she had been dead for between six and ten hours when she was found.'

'Do you have any other remarks that you may have regarding the death of Mrs Carr? For example, did you find any signs on her body that would suggest that she struggled against an unknown assailant or assailants.'

'There were no signs of struggle.'

'Was there anything in the house that suggested a struggle had taken place?'

'No.'

The questioning was remorseless; the direction of the verdict to follow, inescapable. Agatha studied Wilson's reaction to the questions. His manner had slowly changed as he accepted that defeat was inevitable. When the questioning finished and Magilton retired to consider the verdict, Wilson rose and left the inn grim-faced. Agatha was about to follow him outside but then thought better of it.

Instead, she and her friends looked at one another. The lack of any sign of struggle and the existence of the suicide note suggested there was only one conclusion likely, notwithstanding the disappearance of Evelyn Carr. But Agatha was beginning to develop a separate theory on this. A theory so outrageous she could barely bring herself to speak it in front of her friends.

She felt sure that Dr Wilson knew where Evelyn Carr was.

*

They went outside to find the rain falling steadily. Olivia turned to her visitors with a face that seemed unusually downcast.

'Well, I think we can guess what Colonel Magilton's verdict is going to be. No doubt he will turn it into a piece of theatre. I do not propose staying to see his smug face nor suffer to listen to it. I will send the carriage back for you if you do want to stay.'

Agatha answered for the group.

'I don't wish to stay either. I think it's time we returned to London.'

Both Betty and Simpson assented in this. For the moment there was nothing that could be done to influence matters. The group climbed into the carriage and headed back to the estate. They arrived back just before midday. Nobby kindly offered the use of his coach to take the group back to Norwich to catch the late afternoon train to London. Agatha and her friends were happy to take him up on the offer.

'But you'll return for the festival at Hallowe'en?'

Both Agatha and Betty promised they would, but Simpson was more circumspect. He doubted he would be given the time off to come and was faced with the prospect of a weekend without Betty.

They made the four fifty-six train with three minutes to spare and travelled back to London in a subdued mood. However, Agatha's mind was already planning what she would do next. For the moment, her suspicions would remain hers alone. In the meantime, she needed to discount the possibility that Evelyn Carr had escaped or run away. She would deal with this first thing in the morning.

9

Bury St Edmunds, Suffolk: 23rd October 1876

Monday morning and he was late.

Phillip Larwood hated being late. It set a bad example for the office. Where had he put his wallet? Then he remembered. It was in his dress coat. The dinner at the Calder's house. How could he be so stupid? He took the stairs two at a time and stalked over to his wardrobe. It was open. He found the wallet, stuffed it in his pocket and raced down the stairs.

In the entrance hall he saw through the glass in the door and shadow appeared. His heart sank. This was the last thing he needed. Some woman calling collecting for fallen women or some such thing. Did it ever end? Whatever happened to personal responsibility?

He opened the door in a manner he hoped would communicate that he was too busy for such things. There was a way of doing it.

*

The high street of Bury St Edmunds was full and noisy. On one side there was the market. Food stalls ran the length of the street. The smells a wondrous mixture of fresh bread, cooked meat, and horse manure. Street hawkers shouted at ear-splitting levels in the un-ending competition for attention. Men and women and very young children walked in the middle of the street, some stopping at the stalls. Women bargained for every ha'penny as if there life depended on it.

It was Joshua Carpenter who saw him first. Joshua was four years old and even his doting mother worried he was too apt to cling to her. This time she could see why. When she heard him scream her heart froze. She reached down to him, but she could see the terror in his eyes.

'Are you hurt my love? Where?'

But Joshua was pointing to the man. Lettie Carpenter looked up and saw him. Dressed in a smart suit his eyes were staring maniacally ahead. He was staggering like he was drunk. He bumped into a lamp post. Some of the street hawkers saw this and laughed.

Then he came towards Lettie and Joshua Carpenter. She was rooted to the spot. His eyes compelled her to look but not move. She held onto Joshua for dear life. He brushed past them. Lettie spun around to see where he was going.

There were cries on the street from men and women as he bumped into them and strode forward. Someone shouted, 'Phillip.'

Then he disappeared between the stalls. The street hawkers had stopped shouting and an eerie silence descended on the street. Everyone's eyes trained on the spot where the man had disappeared. Then a murmur grew as the men and women discussed what they'd seen. It lasted only a few seconds, though.

Moments later Lettie Carpenter and her boy heard the screams coming from a shop. Terrified screams. Men began running towards the alleyway the man had disappeared. There were shouts now.

Up ahead Lettie saw an old policeman shuffling towards where the shouts were coming from.

There were more screams now. Lettie picked Joshua up and ran away, terrified, from the noise and the commotion.

10

Ignatius Pollaky's Narrative – 24th October 1876

Dames.

Dame Margaret Hopwood to be precise. This dame had kept me up all night and not in a way you would want. Her husband had been caught with hands somewhere they shouldn't be. So, he hired *me* to check on her. What's good for the goose...

But I'm getting ahead of myself. I'm Ignatius Pollaky. Some people call me 'Paddington' on account of my office in Paddington Green. So much for Victorian wit. I'm a private inquiry agent. Just like in the penny dreadfuls. Or not. I haven't read too many of them. The most exciting thing I get to do is prove that your old lady is somebody *else's* old lady. More Bed-Hopping Bertie than *Spring-Heeled Jack*. It pays, though. I bought a house on the infidelity of others. Long may it continue, I say.

But I digress.

It was eleven o'clock in the morning. The sun was shining. Who am I kidding? This is England. In October. The sun won't reappear for another four months. And that's if we're lucky. It was a hard rain outside. Believe me, rain ain't good for business unless you're selling hats or umbrellas. I, on the other

81

hand, am in the trust business. The less of it there is, the more money I make.

I was wearing an old black suit, a grey cravat and shirt that should have been cleaned last week. I was untidy, I smelt worse than a pair of socks and my whiskers needed a trim. I was everything a private inquiry agent shouldn't be when nobility comes to call.

Lady Agatha Aston doesn't make an entrance when she can land on you like a ton of bricks. We had history that lady and me. Not all of it good. I'd helped her solve a murder at her school, saved her life and for that she spent seven years angry at me.

Dames.

Well Lady, in this case.

For all that, I liked her. Probably more than she liked me. She was smart. Smarter than most of the dumb men running the country, running the police, or just running. Every once in a while, in a moment of weakness, or drunken stupor, I thought maybe we could work together. If I had her alongside me then the cases coming my way would have been a cut above the runaway wife or husband. I'm not complaining although a bit of variety would not have gone amiss.

She arrived in my office like a gale force ill wind. I don't know whose appearance was more shocking. Let's just say I wasn't looking my dapper best and the bottle of whisky I'd taken out of my desk drawer was sitting there open with no glass in sight.

'Have you been drinking?' she asked me, eyes fixed on the half empty whisky.

And those were her first words to me. Not 'Good Morning', 'How do you do?'. Nothing so civil. She's something else. I should add, also, she has the way of looking at you. It's like she's cross with you in an amused kind of way. I know she doesn't approve of me, and she knows that I don't really care. So, we're even.

'I have Lady Agatha,' says I. I picked up the bottle and held it towards her, 'Want some?'

This made her frown and me laugh.

'No thank you Ignatius. It's a little early. So, this is your office?' she says looking around. There was enough of a question in there to mask the censure in her tone. She didn't seem impressed, though. Hell, I'm not very impressed by it either.

I felt like saying, how about it sister? You and me. We can take on the world. The underworld that is. I decided not to. I knew what her answer would be. But I suspected a part of her would have loved to say 'yes'.

'Do you like it?' I asked, anyway.

'I think we both know the answer to that Ignatius. Anyway, to business.'

And that's how it started. Just like that. Small talk over. Boom. Business. That's the Agatha I remembered. The one I liked.

'What's on your mind, Lady Agatha?' I said, lighting a cigar.

'Murder, Ignatius.'

'I hope not me. I thought I was forgiven.'

Agatha fixed me with that look. Forty years younger I'd have fixed her one back. What she lacked in height she more than made up for in violence of temper, sharpness of tongue and a very bright pair of blue eyes. Those eyes though. They were set slightly wider apart which made her look more than just smart. I always had the feeling she was laughing at me. Hey, I laugh at

83

me, too. I like that. If she tried, she could have looked like a goddess.

A goddess like Circe.

'For the moment you're safe,' say she, smiling. That's when my senses should have started warning me. But that smile was all female. Like the one that poor sap Adam fell for. I'll say it now, when she put her mind to it, Lady Agatha Aston could teach the ladies down Piccadilly way a few things about flirting. Then she hit me with the sucker punch.

'A woman may have been murdered and it's been made to look like a suicide. Her daughter, meanwhile, has disappeared.'

'What age is the kid?' I asked. Can you believe it? She had me hooked me.

'Eighteen.'

'She's no kid then. What makes you think she didn't kill this lady and then take off.'

This halted Agatha in her tracks and she thought a moment before not answering the question I'd asked her.

'Your job is to find her. I want you to establish that she's not run off to another town or village, God forbid, eloped.'

'Marriage ain't so bad, Lady Agatha. You should give it a try, sometime.'

'Sometime,' said Agatha. The smile reappeared in the form of a frown. I *knew* her, see. Underneath that irritation, sarcasm, and impatience there was a sweet lady trying to get out. Well, not trying very hard mind you.

'What do you want me to do?' I said before blowing out a smoke ring. This didn't impress her as much as it impressed me.

So, she told me.

The Witchfinder General Murders

If only I'd said no. If only I'd listened to my instincts shouting, this lady is trouble. They all are. But no, not me. I'm just a big dope. And so, the trouble began and ended up where it always ends up.

With my innards quaking and someone full of lead.

11

4 Whitehall Place, Scotland Yard: 24th October 1876

Simpson entered through the arch of the imposing red-brick building that housed the Metropolitan Police and went immediately to the first floor to report to Dolly Williamson. The Chief Superintendent of the Detective Branch was in an even more reflective mood than normal as he failed on two occasions to hear Mrs Wickhammersley knock on the door.

'Ah Simpson, you're back. You haven't been tried for witchcraft by our East Anglian cousins then?'

'I don't believe so,' replied Simpson. Williamson laughed out loud leaving Simpson somewhat confused as he'd been telling the truth. He really hadn't been tried for witchcraft.

'So, what transpired at the inquest?' asked the Chief Superintendent.

'I left before the findings were made public,' replied Simpson. This caused a furrow to appear somewhere over the rather bushy brow of Williamson.

'Lady Agatha said there was no point in staying. The magistrate Colonel Magilton was finding for suicide. He'd decided long before the inquest as far as we could tell.'

Williamson nodded and then asked about why Tibbins had suggested in his report that the death may have been under suspicious circumstances. Simpson set the Chief Superintendent right on the police constable but then mentioned Agatha's view of the matter.

'I think that Lady Agatha has some sympathy with the view that this is not straightforward suicide. Unfortunately, there was no evidence that a murder had been committed. There was no sign of a struggle and, of course, there was the suicide note.'

'And the young woman?'

'Lady Agatha said that she would take up this matter, personally. She was rather under the impression that I would be reassigned following the inquest.'

Williamson nodded. Once more this young woman showed an understanding of police investigations that was astute. It was a great pity that the society, never mind the police force, could not avail itself of such intellects.

'As ever, her ladyship is correct. Report to Sergeant Cartwright I believe we have a murder investigation starting. Druscovich is leading it. Cartwright will need some men to go door to door.'

Simpson left the office and went in search of Cartwright. He ran into the sergeant and Chief Inspector Nathaniel Druscovich in the midst of an argument. They silenced when they saw Simpson approach them.

Druscovich was in his mid-thirties. Ambition gleamed from his dark eyes. The youngest Chief Inspector, he was destined for the top, in his opinion. But his rapid rise through the ranks showed that it was a view shared by many. He was the top dog now that Jack Whicher was no longer around. He looked at Simpson coming towards him and smiled. He liked the young policeman. He liked his dog also. Dependability was important in the people who were your subordinates and young Simpson was nothing if not dependable. Nor to be underrated.

'Simpson, what of the case in Norfolk?'

Simpson briefly took him through the detail of what had transpired. Druscovich asked only a few questions. All of them started the same way: 'What did Lady Agatha say about that?'

Simpson felt quite proud that her talents were receiving the recognition that they deserved from someone such as Druscovich. The Chief Inspector nodded thoughtfully as Simpson suggested that Agatha was not prepared to let matters lie. He glanced at Cartwright. Simpson saw this but had no idea what was passing between them. It happened often. Once he'd thought to ask but thought better of doing so.

Druscovich left the two men at this point and Cartwright said, 'Come with me, young man. We've a long day ahead of us. We had a murder or a suicide yesterday.'

'Where did it happen, sir?'

'Bury St Edmonds in Suffolk. Looks like you're on your travels again to East Anglia.'

*

The trip from Kings Cross to Bury St Edmonds took less just under two hours. They were transported from the grey and the decay of London to the clean air, and peaceful surrounds of the country. Simpson viewed the Norman tower of St James' Church as the train pulled in towards the station of Bury St Edmunds.

They were met by Police Constable Royston Elms at the railway station. Elms still looked like the farm labourer he'd been thirty-two years previously. He was not tall but the girth of his shoulders, his paw-like hands and a healthy rosiness to his cheeks didn't so much suggest 'farm' as moo it.

The Witchfinder General Murders

A cab was waiting for them outside the station. Their first stop was the police station to view the body of the dead man.

'His name is Phillip Larwood. He was a lawyer,' explained Elms.

'Family?' asked Cartwright.

'No sir. He wasn't married. I believe there's a brother and two nephews. They've been informed and are coming today to confirm the identification and claim his body.'

The two policemen followed Elms into a room where a body was lying on a table covered with a cloth. Elms pulled back the cloth to his stomach to reveal a deep wound in his gut.

'Can you tell us what happened?'

Elms scratched his head. Cartwright's heart sank. The scratching of a head was always a precursor, in Cartwright's book, to a headache of a case. As ever, Cartwright's instincts were to prove correct.

'Well sir, it's a strange one and no mistake. Mr Larwood walked down the high street. He bumped into several people as he did so. Caused quite a rumpus, he did. A few people wanted to have a go at him. Then he walked into the Jones' Butchers and went to the counter. He reached over and took a large knife that was lying there and calmly stabbed himself.'

Cartwright had been told the outline of the case but had not mentioned it to Simpson. He was intrigued to see what the young man would make of it. He nodded but added nothing to this. He looked at Simpson. It was always good sport to ask the young man his thoughts on any given subject.

'What do you think Mr Simpson?' asked the sergeant.

He smiled when Simpson spoke.

'But this is simply a suicide is it not?' replied Simpson. He did this to hide the fact that he did not have an opinion. No one had cottoned on yet. Reply to a question with your own question was a technique he'd stolen from his old friend Monty.

'We are waiting for a magistrate to be appointed but I imagine this will be the finding,' agreed Elms.

'Have you questioned the witnesses yet?' asked Cartwright.

Elms responded in a manner that suggested he wanted to prove his efficiency to his visitors, 'Only those who were in the shop at the time. I put a notice in the newspaper asking for witnesses to come forward who'd bumped into Mr Larwood on the street. It's clearly suicide, sir. I was surprised when they told me that two gentlemen from Scotland Yard would be coming down to oversee the investigation.'

'Can we speak to any friends or work colleagues of the deceased?' asked Cartwright.

'Yes sir. I can take you to his offices now if you wish.'

'Has anyone come forward who met Larwood on the street?' This was Simpson.

'Yes sir, I have a list of names and addresses here.'

'Very well. Mr Simpson, can you speak to a number of the people on this list? I will meet you back here in two hours. Constable Elms, you will accompany me to the offices of Mr Larwood. We will try and find out more about his state of mind.'

Simpson looked at the little sergeant. It was difficult to warm to the man. There was closeness to him that meant even Simpson found it difficult to trust. Despite the ups and downs of their relationship, he'd much preferred working with the great Whicher. He wasn't sure what he could learn from the sergeant aside from distrusting anyone and everyone. However, in one of the rare moments of insight James Simpson decided to put himself in the shoes of Cartwright. What was he seeing?

The Witchfinder General Murders

A man walks into a shop, picks up a knife and turns it on himself. Despite his relative inexperience, Simpson suspected that such things were unusual. Would this make the verdict certain? No. Not unless there was any new and compelling evidence from his friends or colleagues that suicide was the furthest thing from his mind.

If he was to do his job in the manner that Whicher or, even, Lady Agatha would expect from him, it was important that he assume that Larwood *might* have been murdered irrespective of the manner in which he directly met his end.

For once, Simpson and Cartwright were of a like mind.

*

Two hours later, Simpson returned to the police station having interviewed no fewer than five witnesses who had brushed past or bumped into Larwood on the street. This had taken him to all points of the Bury St Edmunds compass leaving him wearied but quite impressed with the town.

Cartwright's morning had been somewhat easier. A trip to Larwood's offices and then his home, a large house with one male servant and a part time cook. Rather than dwell at the police station, Cartwright suggested they go to the pub and sample the local beer, Greene King, with some lunch.

This suggestion suited Simpson admirably. They parted with Elms and assured him that a report would be sent the next day for the consideration of the magistrate. The two men walked into the centre of the town and found a quaint looking pub with gables, dormer windows, a stagecoach archway that led to a cobbled courtyard. A sign inside the door said Queen Elizabeth I had slept there once.

'I'll bet she did,' said Cartwright, sarcastically. Then again, Cartwright made a morning greeting sound like an exercise in cynicism.

'Oh, do you really think so?' asked Simpson. Cartwright looked at him and hoped he was joking. He could see he wasn't. What on earth had possessed the Chief Superintendent to recruit someone like this? Was the Detective Branch really so desperate?

They sat down and ordered some beer. The pub was filling up with labourers. The beers arrived and they sipped them appreciatively. It had been a busy morning.

'Who have you seen?' asked Cartwright.

'I saw a couple, Mrs and Mrs Stone. Quite elderly. Larwood was unknown to them. They ran into Larwood, or to be more precise, Larwood ran into them. They complained to a constable who was on the high street.

'How did they describe him?'

'This is the interesting thing; all of the witnesses said the same thing. Larwood seemed out of his mind. One lady was with her son. She said he looked deranged. She feared for her son's life.'

'Was he excited or agitated?'

'No, the opposite, in fact. It's as if he were walking in his sleep. His eyes were open and staring straight ahead. He acknowledged no one not even his friends. A Mr Davies and a Mr Colston both knew Larwood and said that they'd called out to him, but he'd ignored them completely even though he only passed within a few feet of them. It was impossible for him not to have heard them.'

Cartwright nodded. It was very strange. His inquiries at his office confirmed Larwood had shown no signs of ill temper or anxiety the previous days or weeks. There was nothing untoward in his behaviour. A conversation with the bank manager had revealed that he was suffering no financial worries. Larwood had few close friends and led a quiet, respectable life. Elms had spoken with two friends that morning. Neither could think of any reason why Larwood would have chosen to take his life never mind in such a bizarre and disturbing fashion. It was all out of character.

'It's quite the mystery,' admitted Cartwright over his second half pint.

'What about his personal papers, sir? Should we look through them?'

'Leave that to the magistrate and Elms. We're not here to solve the case. Yet. We'll return home and write the facts as we have them. Let the magistrate decide what is to be done.'

'Has anyone been appointed yet?' asked Simpson tucking into a meat pie.

'Yes, just this morning,' replied Cartwright. 'According to Elms, the magistrate's not from this town. Apparently, he deals with suspicious deaths. His name is Magilton. Colonel Magilton.'

12

Grosvenor Square, London: 23ʰ October 1876

Agatha eyed her friend closely as she read *The Times*. Her study of her friend turned slowly to frustration and then exasperation. Betty looked up from the newspaper mystified, as ever, by her friend's change in mood. As much as she adored Agatha, the distance between equanimity and steam pouring from her friend's ears could be measures in split seconds. It had always been so. She needed to take a leaf out of Sausage's book. Nothing seemed to upset her except, perhaps, the lack of romance in her life.

'Well, are you going to tell me, or do I have to read your mind like some lady at the end of a pier?' inquired Betty.

'Haven't you seen it?'

'Clearly, I haven't seen whatever it might be otherwise I would have exclaimed "oh look" or "I say" in a bright manner, dear.'

Agatha suppressed a smile and instead maintained her frown.

'You don't have to be sarcastic. Anyway, go to the classified section.'

'First thing I read, usually.'

'Now you are being sarcastic,' said Agatha frowning. Betty quickly fanned the pages. thereby signalling the end of the skirmish. Betty eyes ran up and down the advertisements. Finally, her eyes alighted on one of particular interest. She read it out.

The whereabouts of a young woman is sought. She has been missing since 15th OCTOBER 1876. She hails from the village of Upper Outwell in Norfolk. She is around five feet five in height. Of slim build, dark hair. She is eighteen years old. A REWARD of FIVE POUNDS will be given for information on her whereabouts, provided such information is furnished within three days from today. – I. POLLAKY, Private Inquiry Office, 13, Paddington Green.

'You haven't,' said Betty, twisting the newspaper down and looking at her friend in shock.

'I have,' smiled Agatha triumphantly. 'The advertisement will appear in all main newspapers and in local Norfolk publications. He has also sent letters to lending libraries and asked them to put it up there, too.'

'Well, better him than us, I suppose.'

'My thoughts exactly,' agreed Agatha. 'Unfortunately, it just means we have to sit here and wait for someone to come forward.' Betty eyed her friend archly. Agatha laughed and acknowledged, 'Perhaps not my strongest suit.'

'Five pounds for a reward? You're not exactly pushing the boat out, are you?'

Agatha smiled and shrugged. If Betty didn't know better, it was as if Agatha wasn't expecting anyone to come forward.

'When did you do this?' asked Betty.

'Yesterday when you were out playing golf.'

'Did I tell you how bad I was?'

'You did, dear.'

Betty reread the advertisement and thought it a good idea. Even if it transpired that her mother had taken her own life, it would be good to know that Evelyn Carr was safe and well. It occurred to her briefly, once more, that Evelyn could have murdered her mother, but it seemed so unbelievable that she discounted it. There was little prospect of hearing anything from Pollaky that day. This meant she was, once more, at a loose end. She really did hate the waiting.

Satisfied some momentum had been created, Betty wondered what to do with herself. Usually, the answer was close at hand. She glanced at her golf clubs. They seemed to be beckoning her. Perhaps there was time for a quick nine. Get back on the horse, so to speak. Her form had been poisonous of late and golf is a game that once it grips you it holds on for dear life. Sometimes by the neck.

Without realising it, she began to swing her arms in the motion of a practice swing. Agatha stopped eating her breakfast and stared in fascination at her friend. Finally, Betty became aware of her friend.

'My tee shots,' explained Betty. 'They're killing my game.'

'How terrible for you.'

*

Poor weather persuaded Betty that it would be better to postpone her latest attempt at mastering the unmasterable. She'd treated algebra in much the same way. Instead, she and Agatha decided to take Talleyrand for a walk to the park. There was a slight drizzle and a wind blowing it to a forty-degree angle. It must be said Talleyrand was less than enthusiastic at the prospect of a walk. As they headed away from Grosvenor Square, Agatha spotted a woman walking with her dog.

'Trouble ahead,' said Agatha.

The trouble in question was thirteen inches in height, weighing in at forty-one pounds with a black curly coat. The poodle was coming in the opposite direction. This was Talleyrand's unrequited love. For nigh on a year, he'd seen her walking in the area prompting all manner of Gallic groans from the besotted Basset. There was no time to take evasive action.

Agatha and Betty held their breath as the poodle and its owner approached. Talleyrand, remarkably, seemed unaware of the approach of his lady love. Or, at least, uninterested. This was odd. Perhaps he'd not seen her.

They were now within a matter of feet from one another. The poodle's owner smiled and nodded to the ladies who did likewise. The poodle, meanwhile, increasingly aware that the Basset's attention seemed to be elsewhere began to simper. Talleyrand ignored her. The poodle began to bark. Talleyrand looked the other way. The desperate young lady stopped in her tracks as the unfeeling, unresponsive, and insensitive trifler passed by without so much as woof or a yip. She gave full vent to her anger at the uncaring wretch.

'Is something wrong with Talleyrand?' asked Betty.

Agatha eyed her dog and replied, 'I think it wasn't just the country air that agreed with him.'

*

Simpson arrived at Grosvenor Square later that evening for dinner. His visits were as frequent as they were welcome, but Agatha sensed that this visit had more than a hint of news about it.

'Have you heard anything new from Upper Outwell?' asked Betty as they sat in the drawing room, waiting for dinner to be served.

But the news Simpson had to communicate was even more exciting. He looked at the two ladies. There was a gleam in his eyes that matched his own.

'The verdict was as expected. Suicide.'

Agatha was slightly disappointed by this. Not the verdict. This much she'd expected. It just seemed as if Simpson had something else to tell them.

'Apparently it took Colonel Magilton less than half an hour to reach this view.'

'The man is an ass,' declared Betty. 'Even if it is true, he surely must have had pause for thought on the disappearance of Evelyn Carr.'

Something on Simpson's face gave Agatha hope that this was not the only news. Their eyes met and a smile appeared on the young policeman's face.

'Is there something else?' asked Agatha.

'As a matter of fact, yes. There was a suspicious death in Bury St Edmunds on Monday morning. I went there with Sergeant Cartwright to hear more. A chap called Larwood walked into a butcher's shop, took a knife and stabbed himself to death.'

The two ladies sat up immediately. So did Talleyrand but this was only because he heard the dinner gong ring. The group rose immediately and went to the dining room eager to hear more.

'But this is a suicide is it not?' asked Betty.

'On the face of it yes but when Cartwright and I spoke to witnesses and people who knew him we could find no motive for wanting to take such a dreadful step. In fact, in the moments leading up to his death he was seen by people on the street as if he were walking in his sleep. He was oblivious to friends. In the shop where he topped himself, they all referred to the strange look in his eyes.'

'How odd,' said Agatha.

'There's more, though. You'll never guess who the presiding magistrate for the case is going to be.'

'Colonel Magilton?' asked Agatha.

Simpson felt deflated. He asked Agatha hurtfully, 'However did you guess?'

'It was easy really,' explained Agatha.

'I certainly wouldn't have guessed,' replied Simpson.

Agatha didn't have to turn to face Betty to know that her eyes were burning into her at that moment.

'I don't know any other magistrates,' said Agatha and glanced at Betty, eyebrows raised.

Betty nodded. Crisis over. Simpson decided he'd have another try though. He was game, to give him his due.

'You'll never believe what he said about the case.'

'He thinks it's murder?' asked Agatha in a voice that tried desperately hard to sound neither patronising nor wearied.

'I say, Agatha, you really are on form. Do you play cricket, by any chance?'

Quite how this related to the cases in hand was not something Agatha was prepared to speculate on as she was genuinely fearful of what the answer would say about Betty's sweetheart.

'So, the colonel believes that a death witnessed by a dozen people or more as suicide is murder whereas a hanging, witnessed by possibly one person, who is now missing, was suicide. The good colonel is certainly full of surprises if not sagacity. I wonder why he thinks it's murder.'

The two women turned to Simpson for an answer.

'Actually, I don't know.'

Betty noticed Agatha gripping her fork rather tightly.

'Would be useful if you could find out, James,' said Betty, kindly. Simpson nodded and moments later his notebook was on the table.

'We need to know if this Larwood was a member of any clubs or societies? What were his interests? Could he have had gambling debts? Was there a skeleton in his cupboard that made him do what he did? As I see it,' said Agatha and she noticed Simpson leaning forward at this point, 'if he committed suicide in this manner, he would it throw light on something that he couldn't bring himself to write down. Something that may have been personally embarrassing to him. If he didn't commit suicide and was murdered, then we have to look at the possibility of some kind of poisoning or use of a drug .

'I say, slow down Agatha. A man can only write so quickly.'

'His home will need to be searched thoroughly. Gas poisoning must be considered. Was he visiting a doctor for any complaint that we are not aware of?'

The list continued and by the end, Simpson's hand was so cramped, it could barely lift the fork. However, he'd endured worse in the service of Queen and country. Thankfully, the quantity of the food and the wine consumed ensured the only lasting injury sustained would potentially be to his liver.

13

Grosvenor Square, London: 26th October 1876

There was little in the newspapers the next day regarding the death of Larwood. One by-line in *The Times* and nothing in the *Telegraph*. Such an oversight was never going to pass without comment from Agatha.

'I mean it's not as if a man going into a shop and stabbing himself is a common occurrence. Shameful. But look, they have room to tell us that Princess Beatrice visited a school yesterday.'

Betty was only half listening. She was desperate to get back out onto the golf course and address the problems afflicting her golf game. She was a born optimist and felt sure, every time she stepped onto the tee, salvation was one swing away.

'When will you be back?' asked Agatha who, similarly, was not really listening to the reply.

'Blackheath,' replied her friend stepping out of the front door, bag of clubs in hand.

Agatha looked up as the door closed outside in the hallway. Then she returned to her newspaper. She felt troubled by the Larwood case and actually agreed with that fool Magilton. The problem, as ever, was that she was not involved. Nor was she to be likely asked.

In such situations, the only sensible option is, of course, to give up and crochet. Sadly, Agatha had shown little aptitude for this decidedly feminine activity. She'd always preferred reading, horse riding and hockey, in this order. This saddened her father but delighted her mother which saddened her father even more. Perhaps this was the point.

The more she thought about it, the more it felt as if Larwood had been subject to a phenomenon she'd read about a couple of years ago: hypnotism. The subject of the article was the Scottish scientist, James Braid, who'd pioneered this practice thirty years previously having seen some early French experiments in the field.

Agatha decided to investigate the area further. The only place that might have any papers related to such a subject was the British Library near Kings Cross station. At best she might find an interesting avenue of inquiry, at worst she'd learn about a new scientific endeavour. It did not seem such a bad way to spend a free morning.

*

The Reading Room at the British Library was based on the idea put forward by the Principal Librarian, Antonio Panizzi. It was brought to life by architect Sydney Smirke. Following its opening in 1857 it quickly became a destination for many famous writers and thinkers such as Darwin, Dickens and Marx. Agatha had visited the room on a number of occasions and loved its circular shape and structure with its cast iron, concrete, glass design inspired by the domed Pantheon in Rome.

Agatha settled down after asking a librarian for any books or papers related to James Braid or on the subjects of Mesmerism and Hypnotism. She suspected it would be a long wait. The library, by 1876, had close to six hundred thousand publications. As she was waiting, she saw a small grey-haired man with a beard prowling around the room. He fixed his eyes on her for a few moments. Then he made his way over.

'*Buon giorno*, Lady Agatha,' said Antonio Panizzi. Sir Anthony Panizzi.

'Sir Anthony,' smiled Agatha, 'I see they can't keep you away.'

'Never,' replied Panizzi sweeping an arm around the room. 'They've given up trying.'

'Quite right, too,' said Agatha, moving aside so that the little Italian could sit down.

'May I ask what you are studying now?'

'Hypnotism and mesmerism. Do you know much about these areas?'

Panizzi shook his head and glanced in the direction of his former assistants and said, 'They will find you something soon, I'm sure.'

Agatha looked dubious. She'd come without building her hopes up too much. After all, it was a new field of science. Panizzi seemed amused by Agatha and his smile grew as a few moments later a librarian came clutching two books.

'I'm impressed Sir Anthony.'

The face of Panizzi reddened slightly and he laughed, 'They are copying my system for filing all over the world. We can find anything in a matter of minutes. That's if the person requesting the book gives us enough information. But what are you working on? I remember once you came here asking for books on Toxicology. Not quite what I would have anticipated for a schoolgirl.'

Agatha told him of the two deaths and how they were connected by the same magistrate. Panizzi sat back in his seat and his eyes twinkled. He called over the librarian and wrote down another topic for him to seek out books.

Agatha looked at him suspiciously.

'What did you ask for?'

'You'll see,' said the Italian with a mischievous gleam in his eye.

A few minutes later the librarian returned with half a dozen books. He set them down in front of his former boss.

'There are more, but these are the most popular requests.'

'Thank you, Arthur,' replied Panizzi.

Agatha, meanwhile, was glancing at the books in surprise.

'Witchcraft, Sir Anthony?'

'Witchcraft, Lady Agatha.'

*

The morning spent in the library left Agatha better informed on the history of witchcraft, hypnotism and potential spells that could induce a condition that made the human subject susceptible to suggestion. It came from a German Grimoire dating back to the early part of the century by Protestant pastor Georg Conrad Horst. He had made a study of ancient texts and published a six-volume collection of the magic rites contained therein.

The book owned by the library was the creation of a student who had dispensed with much of Horst's writing and copied out the enchantments as if they were from a recipe book. Agatha's German was not so rusty as to prove equal to the task of understanding the ideas being communicated. Panizzi had left her to her studies and reappeared as she was leaving.

'Have you found what you were looking for?' asked Panizzi.

'To be honest, I don't know. I feel better informed, however, thank you, Sir Anthony.'

Panizzi bowed and Agatha took his arm as he led her out of the Reading Room. Meanwhile the librarian went to the table vacated by Agatha and collected the books. After he had placed them in a trolley for one of his assistants to return to their shelves, he went to the visitors' book.

The policeman had asked him specifically to note the names of those visitors who requested books on witchcraft. He noted Agatha's name and scribbled it down on a piece of paper. Then he added his own notes on the date, time and the books she'd read. He placed the note in an envelope and addressed it.

As he was doing so, he heard Panizzi returning. Lady Agatha Aston was with him. He was saying to her, 'Of course your Lady Agatha it is not a problem in the slightest.'

Panizzi walked over to the librarian and asked to see the visitors' book. He looked at his former assistant and asked him, 'Can you remember who else has asked to look at these books on witchcraft recently?'

'How recently, Sir Anthony?'

The Italian turned to Agatha and raised his eyebrows in the time-honoured fashion.

Agatha replied, 'It depends how many there are. Are these popular books as you say?'

The librarian smiled and said, 'They are not asked for frequently, but they are usually requested by name hence the fact that I could find them so quickly. Let me show you the most recent requestees.'

Agatha borrowed a pen and some paper to note down the names. The first few meant nothing to her. They were all men. This suggested to Agatha that they would either be historians or have some association with Freemasonry. The most recent request from a woman had, in fact been eighteen months previously. Agatha noted her name, Celeste Caradoc. For curiosity Agatha checked the other date that was on the library card against the visitor book. It was from two women.

Mrs O Carr and Miss B Dahlia.

No address was supplied in the visitor book, but none was needed. Agatha changed colour slightly but said nothing. Panizzi noticed the reaction of Agatha.

'Are you well, Lady Agatha?'

'I'm fine Sir Anthony. Thank you very much for a very informative morning. I will see myself out.'

Panizzi and the librarian smiled at Agatha as she walked away. The old librarian noticed the envelope on the table. He didn't have his glasses so could not read the writing. The younger man put the envelope in his pocket and went to find a younger assistant. Panizzi guessed that this was to post the letter. He wondered if the note was related to the unusual request from Lady Agatha.

*

Agatha didn't believe in coincidences. So, Ophelia Carr and Beatrix Dahlia had been to the library. They'd requested books on witchcraft. Grimoires with spells. Dr Wilson had already suggested that Ophelia Carr was a witch. It required little leap in the imagination to believe that Beatrix Dahlia was one, too. The grey, wildly unkempt hair. The rather dignified air. Perhaps the cackle would have been somewhat inapplicable, but she certainly had something about her that suggested witch.

As Agatha thought this she stopped and burst out laughing, causing an elderly couple walking nearby to give her a wide berth. It was ridiculous really. Just a whiff of evidence and already she had tried and convicted the lady of being a witch. Matthew Hopkins would have loved her.

Of course, there were any number of explanations as to why she would have taken the trouble to read such material. However, Agatha was young enough to believe her instincts were unchallengeable. For was instinct nothing more than the aggregation of knowledge, personal observation and experience? Perhaps she was lacking in the latter, but she felt that she had reasonable qualifications in the former two. And arrogance, she thought, causing another outburst of laughter and a policeman to turn sharply towards her.

Upon her return to Grosvenor Square, she was met by a flustered Flack. To be fair this was his normal demeanour. However, on this occasion he seemed even more agitated than normal.

'Good Lord, Flack, whatever can be wrong?'

'Your ladyship, I'm worried about Talleyrand,' replied Flack.

'Why? What's wrong?'

'He seems not to be himself,' explained the butler.

'Really? But why?' asked Agatha. She looked at Flack. His hands were gripping one another tightly. Despite his rather lethargic nature, it was clear that Flack adored the hound. It made Agatha unaccountably happy to see that he cared so much.

'Well, I took him for a walk not one hour ago. He was very happy to take a stroll. On our way back we met that cursed black poodle.'

'And he ignored her?' asked Agatha.

This stopped Flack in his tracks. He'd always known that her ladyship was a little too smart for *his* own good, but this was quite extraordinary.

'Well, yes, your ladyship. Normally...'

Agatha held her hand up, not needing to be reminded how the lovelorn Basset usually reacted when he saw the poodle in question.

'I wouldn't worry about Talleyrand. I think he'll be back to his usual self soon, I'm sure. Now, some tea would be lovely,' said Agatha, effectively ending the conversation.

Flack trooped back to the kitchen relieved he'd done nothing to discommode either her ladyship or the hound. This was not how one achieved the easy life he so desperately sought.

And deserved.

14

British Library, London: 26ᵗʰ October 1876

Sir Antony Panizzi had spent close to forty years working at the British Library. A political exile from his native Italy, he had made a successful life in London. The library's collection of books had more than doubled during his tenure. It was the largest collection in the world, and he'd overseen the introduction of a sophisticated cataloguing system and the building of the Reading Room. As a consequence, the Library had become a popular port of call for the artists and writers in the capital. For his efforts he'd been knighted by the Queen just after his retirement in 1866.

However, he could never quite stay away from the child that he'd helped create. He was a regular visitor if only to keep contact with the various famous people and politicians he'd formed friendships with over the years. And he was very political. Like any good Italian his nature had a vein of suspicion that he could never quite shake off.

A sleepless night had been spent wondering exactly what and to whom his former assistant, Arthur, had written. He was convinced that it related to the arrival of Lady Agatha the books that she'd read on witchcraft. A plan formed in his mind.

Jack Murray

Later that morning he arrived at the library as usual. For the first half an hour he kept one eye on his old subordinate while he chatted with some old friends who'd arrived at the Reading Room. Finally, around midday, his assistant went out of the room for lunch. Panizzi made his excuses and immediately went to retrieve two of the books read by Agatha the previous day. He placed them on an empty table and then wrote the name and address of an old friend who had long since passed on to the great *biblioteca* in the sky.

Half an hour later Panizzi positioned himself near the visitors' book when his old assistant returned. After a few minutes Arthur noticed the new requests in the book. He looked up and around at the room which had emptied considerably. The man who'd requested the books had clearly left. Heavenwards, probably.

Taking some paper and a pencil, the assistant noted down the name and address of the man who'd made the request. He slipped the note into an envelope and addressed it. The little Italian glanced down at the note from a position just behind his old assistant. He could see the name, but the address was difficult to read. That was academic. He recognised the name.

Inspector Druscovich.

*

Afternoon tea had just been served by Flack in the drawing room at Grosvenor Square when the telegram from Panizzi arrived.

The two ladies were as downcast as the weather. Outside, winter had begun to take full effect. Rain beat off the pavement in a manner that dared anyone to venture out. Both Agatha and Betty declined the invitation. The most exciting activity, either lady had to look forward to, was reading '*Sold for Naught'*, a publication that hinted at illicit slave trading, if the scantily clad female in the cage was anything to go by. Betty, meanwhile, was buried in a more serious tome, '*Famous Crimes*', although this latter publication was unlikely to shed any new light on crimes the two ladies were familiar with.

In truth, they were both bored. Bored with London. Bored with the weather and, though they had not openly admitted as much, bored with their lives. At least, reflected Agatha, Betty had her golf and the romance with Simpson. It had been on her mind for some time that she needed to develop an interest. Something that would occupy her time and, more importantly, her mind. Involvement with criminal cases was too irregular. A gap of seven years followed by two fairly close together did not suggest there was a future.

She wondered if following scientific pursuits in the manner of Ada Lovelace might be worth considering. However, the thought of being closeted away in either a laboratory or a classroom held little appeal.

The problem she faced was not just resistance to the idea of women having a larger role in society from men but also a reluctance on the part of women to engage in this struggle. She realised, with some shame, that she fell into this category.

'And Ignatius? Has he made any progress,' asked Betty hopefully. She saw her friend smile enigmatically. This always irritated her and usually acted as a prelude to a volley of abuse. However, this time it was the answer that did it.

'No, not a word,' replied Agatha without a seeming care in the world.

'You don't seem particularly put out by this fact, if I may say,' pointed out Betty in a controlled voice meant to imply I'm-losing-my-temper-here. 'Perhaps if you'd offered six pounds rather than five.'

'Now you're mocking me, dear,' laughed Agatha.

'Me! As if I would ever contemplate such calumny,' exclaimed Betty, who most certainly would. 'What is our plan now?'

'The plan remains the same. We shall solve these cases whether the police want us to or not. Specifically, I thought I would give the advertisements one more day then I'll ask Mr Pollaky to up the reward to something more tempting.'

They settled into a comfortable silence. Betty studied her friend. She was gazing out of the window, but her eyes did not seem to have any focus. It was as if she were seeking inspiration. Betty felt a little guilty for her outburst earlier.

'Are we any nearer solving the case yet, then?'

Agatha smiled grimly and replied, 'Oh to have the opportunity. We either need a break in the case or an excuse to become involved.'

It is a strange and often true phenomenon in life as well as in elevated literary tomes that such thoughts are accompanied by the very thing which the speaker has, just that moment, asked for.

There was a knock at the door which was ignored by Talleyrand and eventually answered by Flack. Soon he brought in the Panizzi telegram thereby re-energising an otherwise sleepy afternoon in the Grosvenor Square household.

'Good Lord,' exclaimed Agatha as she read the communication. 'That's interesting.'

'What is?' asked Betty looking up from '*Famous Crimes*'.

'I told you about my trip to the library yesterday, well it transpires that the librarian there was under instruction to inform a certain person of whomsoever should request the books that I did.'

'Who asked for this?'

'Our old friend Druscovich from Scotland Yard.'

'I say,' said Betty.

*

The arrival of Simpson at Grosvenor Square for the first time in a couple of days was greeted with a gratifying amount of excitement as far as the young policeman was concerned. In truth, he'd found the last few days trying and not solely because he was away from his lady love. Over dinner they shared their news.

'Colonel Magilton has recorded an open verdict on the death of Larwood. To say that Druscovich is angry about this is an understatement.'

'Does this mean you cannot officially close the case?' asked Betty with a grin.

'Correct. Nor can we investigate it unless new evidence comes to light, however. This nettled Druscovich, of course.'

'The colonel has a nerve,' replied Agatha. 'I don't disagree with his verdict in this case. It makes eminent sense but not to have taken a similar view on the death of Mrs Carr given some of the unanswered questions strikes me as perverse.'

They retired to the dining room for dinner and Agatha updated Simpson on her findings from the library.

'Druscovich requested this? Do we know when?'

Agatha shook her head and fixed her eyes on Simpson.

'You will have to ask him.'

Simpson looked unhappy at this but realised that this was inevitable. If it was material to the investigation that he needed to know what avenues of inquiry were still open.

'And what do you make of Ophelia Carr and Beatrix Dahlia looking at books on witchcraft, Agatha?'

'And hypnotism, don't forget. It's all together a very strange situation. It makes one wonder about Miss Dahlia. I mean, let's be honest, she could easily be mistaken for a witch.'

Both Simpson and Betty erupted into laughter notwithstanding the fact that they knew Agatha was not joking. Only Agatha was capable of saying the unsayable and making it seem as if it was axiomatic, thought Simpson. If only men had such freedom.

'I think when we go back to Upper Outwell we should speak to Miss Dahlia and find out more,' said Agatha ignoring her friends.

'I'm sure you'll see Dr Wilson again,' suggested Betty in manner that was pregnant with meaning. Agatha looked at Betty causing her friend's hopes to plummet.

'Oh, have you lost interest in our Byronic doctor?'

'I was never interested, dear. Anyway, I didn't say at the time, but I have a suspicion that Dr Wilson not only harbours feelings for Evelyn Carr, but he also knows where she is.'

'But why didn't you say anything?' asked Betty. In fact, she was asking why Agatha had specifically not said anything to her. Agatha felt a stab of guilt at this so ignored the question entirely and, instead, shared her thinking on the case.

'I think that Evelyn Carr was there the night her mother was murdered. I think she is in hiding from the murderer. Dr Wilson knows this but is reluctant to risk the life of Miss Carr, hence my suspicion that his interest is more than just that of a disinterested friend. Unfortunately, he had no other proof to introduce to the inquest aside from the testimony of Miss Carr.'

'But why wouldn't both Dr Wilson and Evelyn Carr want to testify to the murder and see an investigation to catch the killers.'

Agatha sat back and frowned.

'I've thought about this a lot. The only thing that occurred to me is that she did not see the killers or the murder. Perhaps she was in hiding when they came. I don't know. The whole thing throws up too many questions and I have no evidence to speak of or any way of speaking to the key participants. All I have is conjecture and an over-active imagination. While you're writing, James, can you find out about Miss Celeste Caradoc. She was another name that the librarian sent to our friend, Druscovich.'

Both ladies turned to Simpson. His notebook was out, and he was scribbling away with his pencil. Finally, he looked at Agatha and said, 'Sorry, what came after Dr Wilson has no proof to introduce?'

15

Ignatius Pollaky's Narrative – 27th October 1876

I'm a dumb sap. Always have been. I never learn where the ladies are concerned. When Lady Agatha came calling, I should have gone running. She's a good kid. A little too smart. But the set up was all wrong. I should have seen it from the start.

To begin with no one, *nessuno, nadie* responded to the advertisement. No, that's not quite true but we'll come on to that. My case with that other dame had finished and the only thing I had to entertain myself was lying in the bottom drawer of my desk.

Anyone who thinks being a private detective is full of bullets, broads and, well let's not go there, is full of it. Let me tell you, it's all waiting, watching and writing. Waiting outside hotel rooms, watching a man or a woman being in a place they shouldn't be with someone they are absolutely not supposed to be with and then the sad husband or wife writing you a cheque.

It's a living, though.

But not much. Maybe I was angry that day. I spat out curses that filled the office. Give me come excitement, I said. A dead body would be good. Well, not if that dead body is me. I draw the line at that, buddy, I can tell you.

The Witchfinder General Murders

The case was going nowhere faster than a hansom cab being pulled by a Derby winner. That kind of fast. So, I called on Lady Agatha to give her the dope.

Her place is bigger than Basingstoke. Never been to Basingstoke. Don't want to if you take my meaning. That decrepit old duffer Flack answered the door with all of the welcome and cheery bonhomie of a groom visiting his wife's mother for the weekend.

At least Agatha can make you feel at home. When she puts her mind to it, that is. Other times she can freeze you like a nor' wester in Murmansk.

'Has our advertisement produced a response?' she asks me.

'No,' says I. Oh boy, did I ever speak to soon. The thing is she didn't seem that surprised. It was like she knew no one would have seen the missing broad. Then I asked her, 'Do you want me to increase the reward?'

'No, I don't think we need to do that, Ignatius,' she said. I tried to argue with her, but she was having none of it.

Oh, you fool, Pollaky. Oh, you fool.

Then she said I should go out to Upper Outwell and ask around.

I said, 'It's your money but I can tell you, it will be a waste of time. I know these villages. They don't talk about their own to people like me. If you hadn't noticed I'm an outsider. Worse, I'm foreign.'

She was having none of it. She said we needed to try at least. For the sake of the girl. Eighteen years old. Alone. Lost her mother. Oh, she laid it on all right. The only thing missing were the violins.

Later that evening is when all the trouble began. I went back to the office at Paddington Green. There was no post. No telegrams. No new job aside from what Lady Agatha had asked me to do. And I was going to go out to that godforsaken village the next day. I thought I'd call it a day. I locked up the office and went outside. Then I felt it.

Cold steel.

My pulse quickened. Something else was loosening. That concentrated my mind somewhat.

'One move,' says he, 'And I paint the pavement with your throat.'

I said, 'Don't do anything we'll both regret.'

He laughed at that and told me to put my arms behind my back. As I'd nothing better to do at that moment I did. He slipped the hand cuffs on me like he'd done it before. Then he put a hood over my head and marched me to a cab and we were off.

I've no idea where we were going but it wasn't a long trip. Next thing I knew I was out of the cab and being pushed towards something. I was worried it was the river. Was this it for 'Paddington' Pollaky?

Clearly not. I was led into a house. I didn't go up the stairs. Instead, he pushed me straight into a room. The hood stayed on. The cuffs stayed on. His hand on my shoulder forced me into a seat.

'White no sugar,' says I.

They didn't get the joke.

Then I heard a noise. There was another person in the room. I could hear the two of them whispering. The second man spoke. If I was scared before I heard this man, then I felt like crying when he began.

The Witchfinder General Murders

His voice was low and deliberate, but you could tell immediately that he was a man who knew death, who'd inflicted death and who felt no remorse for having done so.

'Mr Pollaky,' said the demon, for it was a demon. The words cut through the air like a knife slicing through flesh. 'You placed an advertisement in the newspaper the day before yesterday. What response have you had?'

'None,' says I.

'Speak up Mr Pollaky, I can't hear you,' said the voice.

'Take the damn mask off me and then you will,' I shouted. I hoped my voice didn't sound as scared to him as it did to me. He said nothing to that, so I said, 'None.'

'I don't believe you.'

I let him know what I thought of his thoughts on the subject. I received a dig in the ribs as a reward. Call it a feeling, well, it had to be a feeling, but I thought that he wasn't going to kill me. At least not yet.

No, he had something worse in mind, as I was about to find out.

I sensed the chair he was sitting on being pulled closer to me. He was barely a few feet away. Even with the mask I could hear the sound of his breathing.

'Mr Pollaky, your righteous anger is really fear. I understand this. So, do you. But I don't think you are fearful enough. So, let us suppose for a moment that you are telling me the truth. Let us suppose that no one is coming forward. Let us further suppose that Evelyn Carr is in hiding. Or that someone is hiding her. I want to find her. I want you to find her. Now, I know that you have a client. Lady Agatha Aston, I understand, is most desirous that you locate Miss Carr.'

119

As he appeared to know I saw no reason to deny it. Then he continued on that low voice which was making my bowels quake.

'I am, too. However, the rate that I will pay you is much higher than Lady Aston's. It does not involve money. You are married are you not? Mary Anne, isn't it? You have a young family. A son. Three daughters. I think my meaning is clear, isn't it, Mr Pollaky? I will spare you but not your family. Find Evelyn Carr. Bring her to me. Do not speak to anyone of this meeting or I will carry out my threat. You will, of course, be followed. I will know immediately if you try to disobey this order.'

Then I had to ask, didn't I?

'What do you want me to do with this kid?'

'Kill her, Mr Pollaky. Kill her and bury her body by the oak tree at her house. A shallow grave will suffice. You have until the first of November.'

That was less than a week away.

16

Grosvenor Square, London: 28ᵗʰ October 1876

'I see Ignatius has put a new advertisement in *The Times*,' said Betty.

This seemed to surprise Agatha and then she shrugged it off. She hadn't told him not to increase the reward and perhaps he felt it was time to create some momentum. She hadn't shared with him her thinking behind the advertisement. Why should she? Where Ignatius was concerned, it was best that he was kept on a short leash.

'I suppose he's increased the reward,' said Agatha, looking up from the *Telegraph*.

'Yes, he's put it up to six pounds. That will have them queuing up along the park. He seems in a bit of a rush. Look at the date he's put down.'

Now Agatha was confused. She stood up and walked around to Betty so that she could see what Pollaky had written. The advertisement was, for the most part, similar to what had been written before:

The whereabouts of a young woman is sought. She has been missing since 18ᵗʰ OCTOBER 1876. She hails from the village of Upper Outwell in Norfolk. She is around five feet four in

121

height. Of slim build, dark hair. She is eighteen years old. A REWARD of SIX POUNDS will be given for information on her whereabouts, provided such information is furnished within ONE day of today. SEE BELOW - I. POLLAKY, Private Inquiry Office, 13, Paddington Green

Agatha studied the advertisement for a few minutes until an exasperated Betty made enough movement and sounds to suggest that it was her paper and she wanted to move onto something else. Even then Agatha stood for a few moments longer than Betty found she could tolerate, Finally, she returned to her seat and asked her friend what she was doing today.

"I think I shall try and get nine holes in.'

In practice this meant anything between eighteen and thirty-six holes as Betty sought to recapture the form which had, recently, deserted her.

'And what about you dear?'

Agatha smiled and buttered some toast then added a generous topping of orange marmalade.

'Just a few odds and ends I've been meaning to clear up and I want to catch up with an old friend. Who are you playing with?'

Betty turned down the corner of the paper and glanced at her friend.

'Lesley Chadderton,' responded Betty before shrugging and returning to her paper.

*

Meanwhile, with his latest notebook now full to the brim, Simpson made his way into Scotland Yard with but one thought in mind. How would he respond to the latest carpeting? In truth, getting hauled over the coals was not something that worried him unduly. It had been an almost daily occurrence when he was at school. Perhaps if he'd been more academic...

This theme continued well into his days as a cavalry officer. It was his essentially easy-going nature which made him such a natural target for those of a more martinet-like disposition. Such is the way with bullies. He neither took offence at censure nor, to be fair, did he learn from it. This contributed to a cycle that seemed to repeat itself all too frequently. The positive from it all was that he developed a rather thick skin. As he skipped up the steps to the first floor his challenge was less about the inevitable explosion from Druscovich and more, as Agatha had pointed out, how he could prove one way or another that Druscovich was not up to his eyes in this mess.

Epiphanies were a rare phenomenon in the life of James Simpson. If they happened at all, it was because he, briefly, could picture how someone smarter than he might approach a problem. Great thoughts that were borne from his own prognostications or moments of inspiration were rarer, as the saying goes, than teeth on a *galus domesticus.*

'Sergeant Cartwright,' said Simpson in a manner that the shrewd sergeant realised was not a greeting but a request to speak to him. This was unusual as Simpson's normal address to him was a cheery 'what ho'.

Simpson took Cartwright to one side. For a few minutes the sergeant listened to what Simpson had to say on the subject of Druscovich. The mention of Agatha had nearly derailed the process before he'd had an opportunity to explain himself. Thankfully, Cartwright had kept his temper in check long enough to hear the full story. And it was quite a story which he finished by mentioning the need to find out about Celeste Caradoc.

The latter question was more easily answered.

The two men went to their desks while Cartwright considered what to do about Druscovich as well as the fact that the meddling young noblewoman was connecting witchcraft to the hanging in Upper Outwell. It seemed clear to him that no good could come of this. To be more precise, no good could come of him being seen to tolerate any connection between Druscovich and malpractice, although he had his suspicions on this front. As regards the story of witchcraft it seemed too fantastical. But nor could he ignore it. Just because something was unlikely did not mean it could not have happened. They needed proof.

Cartwright had a reputation in the force for making a fox look like a blithering ingenue, this native guile came to his aid now. He called Simpson over.

'Go to the library and ask for some books on witchcraft. Make some play about reading them. In fact, better still, if this man Panizzi is there, introduce yourself and find out who the librarian is. No point in going to this trouble and he's having a day off. Assuming he's there and proceeds to send a note to Druscovich, intercept the letter, or have Panizzi do this. One other thing, Simpson.'

'Yes?' smiled Simpson.

In a tired voice Cartwright said, 'You will use an assumed name, won't you?'

'Ah, good idea, sir,' replied Simpson.

Simpson noticed that Cartwright seemed all of a sudden quite weary and he was shaking his head. He was about to ask if he was feeling well when he thought better of it. Instead, inspired by his own good thinking, he rose from his seat and decided to strike while the iron was warming up nicely.

The Witchfinder General Murders

*

Simpson arrived at the British Library Reading Room just after ten in the morning. It was his first visit and there was an air about the place that he quite liked. With something approaching embarrassment he realised he'd never been a great reader. The classics had bored him immensely. He quite liked some Shakespeare, Henry V and what not, but much of it left him cold. The only thing he returned to with anything approaching enthusiasm were the penny dreadfuls which he consumed with as much relish as he did food. And he liked his food.

Panizzi was not difficult to spot. He went to the desk and made his request and waited for the little Italian to join him. Sure enough, upon hearing the request, Simpson became aware of Panizzi sitting down near him. He was smiling broadly.

'A very interesting request, sir,' said Panizzi smiling. 'We shall have your books in a few minutes.'

Simpson smiled back at the former Principal Librarian.

'Actually, I'm not really interested in them at all. Lady Agatha sent me, Sir Anthony.'

Panizzi's eyes twinkled with delight. He glanced towards the desk and then back to the young man.

'My name,' explained Simpson, 'is not what I wrote on your visitors' book. I'm Simpson. I'm with the Detective Branch at Scotland Yard. Chief Inspector Druscovich is my senior officer.'

'Has he sent you?'

'No. He doesn't know I've come. I hope we can keep it this way.'

Panizzi bowed by way of response. Then he leaned forward and said, 'That man behind the desk with the moustache is the

Chief Librarian, Arthur Stebbins. I believe he is sending these notes to your Inspector in good faith.'

Even for Simpson the meaning was clear, and he liked the Italian all the more for his desire to look after his former colleagues from the library. He nodded to Panizzi and they both waited for the librarian to write his note.

While they were waiting, Simpson decided to leaf through the grimoire. It contained various spells each less interesting than the last. The book contained not only spells but descriptions of the ingredients that were important for incantations. It certainly provided a new slant on gardening for the young policeman.

Finally, the librarian became aware of the latest request. He looked around for a piece of paper and took a pencil from his pocket. Simpson was about to rise when he felt a hand on his arm.

'Let me,' said Panizzi. 'Meet me outside.'

Simpson rose from the desk and went outside while Panizzi ambled over to the librarian's desk. He glanced down at the envelope.

'I was just going to the post office. Do you want me to send this for you?' asked Panizzi to Arthur.

He felt oddly nervous or perhaps it was guilt. He desperately wanted that his former assistant was not involved in something irregular, criminal even. He was greeted with a smile.

'That's very kind of you, Sir Anthony. Are you sure?'

'Of course, old fellow. I was just on my way.'

Relief coursed through the veins of Panizzi and he took the envelope and marched outside. He spied Simpson standing at the entrance. He showed Simpson the envelope. It was addressed, as the other had been, to Inspector Druscovich.

Simpson was just about to say that this must have been an old request because the man in question had been promoted many times since his days as an Inspector. Then he spotted the address.

'Good Lord,' said Simpson.

Panizzi looked concerned. All his fears returned that his man was up to no good. This fear increased when Simpson tore the envelope open. He looked at the note. It read:

Dear Inspector, Druscovich,

Another request for the books you asked me to make a note of. It is from Mr B. E. Nick, c/o Pentonville Street Mansions. The date is as marked.

Yours

Panizzi was concerned on a number of levels now, not the least was the fact that a letter he'd committed to posting had been tampered with. He looked at Simpson for an explanation. Simpson saw the concern on the old librarian's face.

'I fear you colleague has been taken in. This letter was never meant for the Inspector. I must report this.

'What shall I tell Stebbins?'

Agatha's instructions on this had been crystal clear. So much so that she had to repeat them twice as Simpson hadn't quite grasped what she meant.

'I would suggest saying nothing for the time-being. No harm can come of it. Anyway, there is every chance that someone may come along and ask him to change the addressee.'

'How do you know?' asked Panizzi still baffled.

'I know because the address belongs to someone entirely different,' responded Simpson.

'Who?'

'Someone who's dead,' responded Simpson.

*

Simpson returned immediately to Scotland Yard to report his finding. He wasn't sure what it meant but it was good news on two fronts. He and Cartwright were off the hook for implicating a superior officer in a crime. It also gave them grounds for him to continue his involvement in the case.

'What does your friend think?' asked Cartwright when Simpson had informed him. He was clearly referring to Agatha.

'I don't know, sir. I came here first,' replied Simpson.

This seemed to surprise the sergeant. For, perhaps, the first and probably only time he wished that the young man had gone to Lady Agatha first. This would have presented him with the delicious prospect of tearing a strip off Simpson whilst benefitting from the unquestionable wisdom of the noblewoman.

'When you finish writing your report, I suggest that you find out what your friend thinks. Don't submit the report, however. We need more on this before the Chief Inspector hears tell of what we've been up to.'

This was an altogether excellent suggestion. He looked at the sergeant who still seemed to be cogitating on the subject.

'We may need to go back out there again.'

'Where?' asked Simpson. The sergeant exhaled slowly.

'Norfolk.'

'Ahh,' replied Simpson as light entered the dark echoey confines of his cranium. 'I know Lady Agatha is intending to return to Upper Outwell for the village Hallowe'en festival. I think she's going this weekend. Perhaps we could kill two birds with one stone.'

*

'Larwood?' exclaimed Agatha. She'd always suspected that Druscovich was a ruse, but this was a surprise.

'Yes, I was in his house only a few days ago so I recognised the address immediately.'

Betty looked at Agatha and then at Simpson. Agatha sat back in the sofa and exhaled slowly. It was late afternoon in Grosvenor Square. Simpson had gone first to Scotland Yard to update Cartwright on the development. The reaction of the sergeant had not been so very different from Agatha's. Perhaps there was some relief too from Cartwright. The thought of confronting Druscovich had not been high up on the list of things he wanted to do at that point in his career.

Agatha confirmed what had been on Simpson's mind: the open verdict for Larwood's death meant that the case was not officially closed. They now had something else with which they could work.

'Did you ask Sir Anthony to make sure any future correspondence was forwarded?'

Simpson's beaming smile confirmed that this scheme was now in place. This might yet yield an answer if someone came to change the address.

When Simpson told the ladies that he had been given permission to accompany the two ladies and that they also visit Bury St Edmonds he received a well done from Agatha and something more tangible from Betty.

'This good news,' said Agatha. 'We need an ally on the police force. It seems Mr Cartwright might be just the man to have on our side.'

Simpson was less sure of this idea but smiled gamely. It was best not to disagree with Agatha. He was happy to leave that to Betty. Women understood the rules of engagement better than he did.

17

9 Portsdown Road, London: 30ᵗʰ October 1876

Portsdown Road was a respectable if not particularly exclusive street in the Maida Vale area of London. The road was a few minutes away from Regents Park in the centre of London. It was here that Ignatius Pollaky lived with his wife and four remaining children. Three others had been born and lost.

The morning was crisp-cold and bright. The trees on the road stood leafless and naked, frost glistening in the sunlight. A number of pedestrians ambled along the road. One in particular caught the attention of a few. He was tall, ugly and looked very out of place on this street. He went up the pathway to number nine and rapped on the door.

No answer.

He rapped again. This time harder. Irritation strengthened his wrist. The sound of the metal clacking against metal echoed around the inside of the house like rifle shots.

*

Whoever was at the door was going to get an earful. Some of those raps would have taken a weaker door of its hinges, thought Mary Ann Pollaky. She strode to the door with but one thought in mind. Someone was going to get an earful, all right.

A shadow appeared at the stained-glass window panel of the door. All at once Mary Ann felt winter's chill. The shadow was large, dark and as welcoming as a black cloud. Mary Ann could hear the maid upstairs and the sound of children laughing.

She took a deep breath and opened the door. Her eyes met the chest of the visitor. She looked up at the visitor. It was an awfully long way up. He was at least six feet five. There was no smile of greeting from him either. Mary Ann Pollaky turned pale. Whoever he was, he was not welcome. She thought of her children playing inside.

'Mrs Pollaky,' said a coarse voice. 'Is your husband here today?'

The answer to this was 'no'. Pollaky was away to book his train ticket to Norfolk. A case he said. Normally his cases were garden-variety love affairs. One look at the gentleman standing on her doorstep told her that Pollaky was involved in something infinitely more perilous.

How to answer though? By admitting that he was not here the brute before her may take advantage of the situation and try and gain entry. But if she lied, would he stick around and wait for him?

Imperiousness is a valuable weapon to have in one's arsenal. To be effective it must be accomplished with utmost conviction. When done so, it can give even the most bullying of individuals pause for thought.

Mary Ann Pollaky was no one's idea of a shrinking violet. Years of marriage to Pollaky had ensured her skin had thickened every bit as much as *his* waistline. Her initial shock at seeing the visitor had slowly turned to anger. How dare he attack their front door so violently.

'He's at work,' replied Mary Ann glaring at the visitor. She'd decided he was not likely to be a client so restrained irritation was to be the approach.

'Are you on your own Mrs Pollaky?' His voice was soft now as if he was trying not to scare her. Nature, alas, was working against him. His height, his attire, his unshaven features were never going to work on his side.

'What is it to you? State your business, sir or leave.'

A slow smile spread across the man's face. Behind Mrs Pollaky a young child descended the stairs. A boy around ten years of age.

'Mama, who is it?'

'Back upstairs Francis,' replied Mary Ann without turning around. Her eyes were fixed on those of the unknown visitor.

'Is everything all right mamas?'

'I won't tell you again, Francis.'

Mary Ann heard the sound of the young boy climbing the stairs again. The visitor and Mrs Pollaky were, once more, on their own.

'Tell Ignatius that I called,' said the visitor. His voice was harder. 'He knows why.'

With that he turned about and left Mary Ann standing in the doorway trembling from more than just the cold.

Holbrigg Hall, Norfolk: 29[h] October 1876

Nobby's carriage was outside the station at Sheringham. Three travellers trooped wearily onto the carriage for the last leg of their journey. Talleyrand, on the other hand, bounded onto the carriage like a pup going to a puppy party. Betty shook her head, utterly perplexed by Talleyrand's evident enthusiasm. The Basset then proceeded to spend the entire journey with one head stuck out of the window, wind blowing in his face, ears flopping like giant wings, drinking in the fresh Norfolk air. Any attempt by Agatha to close the carriage window was met with an uncharacteristic seditiousness on the part of the normally disconsolate-looking hound. This manifested itself in a growl followed by a pathetic whining.

The choice between freezing in the carriage and listening to Talleyrand's bleating was not so difficult and the human passengers suffered in silence all the way to the estate of their friend while the hound's paws rested on the window of the carriage watching the Norfolk countryside roll by.

When Holbrigg Hall came into view, Talleyrand's excitement grew to a level that was unprecedented in either Agatha's or Betty's experience. He began to bark happily, his tail swinging like the door of an unlatched outhouse in a gale.

'Good Lord,' said Betty. 'What on earth is wrong with him?'

Agatha looked archly at her canine companion and said mysteriously, 'Whatever indeed.'

Ten minutes later the carriage pulled up to the front of the hall and Nobby opened the door to greet his visitors, face beaming with pleasure. As the door opened, Talleyrand flew out onto the path and disappeared at a speed few, least of all his owners, would have believed him capable.

'I say,' said Betty.

Nobby said something that meant roughly the same before looking enquiringly at Agatha. Coincidentally both Betty and Simpson did likewise.

'Perhaps he's gone to see his friends,' suggested Agatha with an ingenuous smile. This explanation was taken as the truth and everyone moved towards the house discussing how wonderfully well Talleyrand had taken to life on the estate.

Olivia came out to greet the visitors dressed like she was about to attend a ball. Her long black gown trailed along the ground and she gestured expansively, 'It's so good to have you back.'

The previous weekend had helped inure Agatha and Betty to the more idiosyncratic excesses of Nobby's wife although even Simpson openly admitted to finding her a bit much. She led the visitors inside chattering away about the evening she'd planned ahead. In truth the visitors would have preferred a quiet and early night after their travels, but it seemed that Lord Burnham and his wife could only visit on this night, so all had been settled.

Agatha and Betty offered up brave smiles in response. They were guests after all. Perhaps visits from people of similar rank were all too rare for Burnham who had an estate to the east of the county. Neither Agatha nor Betty had met the couple before and knew very little of them.

Nobby confirmed that they would have the carriage for the next day to take them to Bury St Edmunds to interview people connected to the late Mr Larwood. Then there was the Hallowe'en festival on Tuesday which all were looking forward to immensely. It was going to be quite a few days on the estate.

*

Talleyrand shuffled into the library an hour later and promptly collapsed on the floor by the French doors. Agatha observed the arrival of her hound with grim amusement. Then she turned to Nobby and asked him how preparations for the festival were going.

'Wonderfully well. Not that I do much. All I have to do is to arrive. Sober, ideally. Say a few words of welcome and declare the whole thing open.'

'I'm sure you do more than that, Nobby,' said Betty.

'He really doesn't,' confirmed Olivia in the manner that all wives learn to do from the moment they declare they'll love, honour and obey their husbands.

Agatha asked if she could be given a tour of the house. On their previous visit there had been too little time to enjoy hearing more about the history of the house.

'I'd be delighted,' said Nobby and they set off after a revitalising tea and scones had been consumed.

'The house was built around the time of Charles I,' said Nobby as he led them along the corridor to the west wing that was mostly shut off. 'Our family were great Royalists and supported Charles up to but not including the moment he lost his crown. It was a bit of a balancing act I gather but we managed to change sides just in the nick of time. My great,

great, well you get the idea, it was a long time ago, his brother had been despatched early in the conflict to play on the other side. I believe on racecourses it's called hedging. Anyway, we had a foot in both camps and managed to step over to the right one just as the axe fell so to speak. Of course, this being Norfolk the whole show was confused by the fact that we had our witch hunts.'

'Did your family participate much in these?' asked Agatha, as they walked along a long corridor containing the previous earls and countesses.

'No, we're a family that have always played both sides,' replied Nobby, stopping by a portrait of a man with long hair but the garb of a puritan. 'This is William. He built this house. Of course, it was added to over the years, but he was the first.'

The William in question looked to be the product of years of refined breeding. His chin was large, and his eyes seemed to droop. Perhaps the artist had caught him on a particularly trying day.

'Not much to look at, the old boy,' admitted Nobby. 'I'd like to think we later Bodkin-Browns have become a more attractive proposition for our betters.' He gave Olivia a friendly pat on her bottom as he said this.

'I say,' said Simpson, looking the portrait situated opposite to William.

Nobby left, 'Yes, the old boy did well, I must say. That's Teresina, my whatnot grandmother.'

The ladies crowded round the portrait. The young woman was strikingly beautiful. All of a sudden, their interest in the ladies who married into the family increased enormously. They looked along the line of portraits of the women. One after another was as beautiful as the last.

The impact in the male inheritor was certainly beneficial as each succeeding ancestor of Nobby's exhibited a marked improvement in appearance on the original patriarch of the family.

'I seem to have inherited my ancestor's taste in beautiful women,' said Nobby proudly. Olivia beamed at the compliment. 'Have you noticed...?'

'They all have black hair,' said Agatha, finishing the sentence. 'And you are right Nobby, the ladies are very beautiful. None more so than you my dear, Olivia.'

It was an odd fact that many of the compliments bestowed by Agatha, as Betty well knew, were in fact malicious insults to those too fatuous to realise that Agatha was sporting with them. However, in this instance, it was clear that the compliment was truthful, sincerely stated and not without a degree of wonder.

Nobby continued his history of the ancestors which became more of a story of the growth of Britain as a colonial nation. One after another of the ancestors through to Nobby himself had served in the British Army. Nobby was the first to acknowledge the family's remarkable ability to survive the various conflicts in which Britain had become involved was a tribute either to rank, a natural predisposition towards avoiding buckshot and spears or just pure luck. Agatha noted the exchange of looks between him and his wife as he said this.

'This is my father Rupert,' said Nobby. There was a slight catch in his voice. Olivia placed a hand on his arm.

Like Nobby he was an odd combination, as the later Bodkin-Brown men had become, of dashing rogue and English squire. Dark hair and a dangerous glint in the eye fought with the admittedly less prominent, Bodkin-Brown jaw. The result was inconclusive but a vast improvement on the original.

'He died a few months before we were married. You remember him of course.'

Agatha remembered him all right. He was as affable as his son and genuinely agreed, by all who knew and liked him, to have had the morals of a particularly dissolute alley cat. All eyes turned to the picture opposite.

Deirdre, his wife, had proven to be the one exception to the rule that Bodkin-Brown wives should be raven-haired beauties. She was ash blond and no one's idea, least of all hers, of being a direct continuation of the line of countesses who'd preceded her. She was, however, very wealthy and the Bodkin-Brown line had reached a point in its evolution when an urgent economic injection took priority over the family tradition.

Ever the soldier, Rupert took his orders and formed a very happy attachment to his wife. The arrival of Nobby gave Deirdre everything she wanted. By a happy coincidence it also released Rupert to follow his own inclinations. Far and wide as it turned out. Across the Indian sub-continent as well as, more locally, in Norfolk, the Earl proved heroically prolific although the marriage itself only produced one son and a daughter.

After the passing of her husband, Countess Deirdre had found love with an Italian count and was now living happily, with her son's blessing, in a villa near Lake Como. Nobby was too agreeable, too sympathetic an individual to begrudge his mother a second chance at happiness after her lord and master had expired earlier than his three score and ten.

'You're the image of her, Nobby,' said Agatha, not sure if this was a compliment or a slight but certainly what everyone was thinking.

'Yes, two peas, what?' said Nobby with a broad grin.

Jack Murray

Dinner with Lord Burnham was set for eight that evening. The tour of the mansion left around an hour for the ladies to get ready and for the men to take up their billiard cues once more.

A more refreshed Agatha was looking forward to meeting Lord Burnham. Unlike many of his class he had chosen an academic life and was a noted medieval scholar. Not many papers had been published on the period, even fewer read.

At the appointed hour, the guests arrived. In appearance, Lord Burnham was everything Agatha had expected and more. Grey of hair, ruddy of cheek and fecund of whisker. His smile was expansive, starting out from somewhere in East Anglia. And why not? He was as fit as any man of sixty-two should be.

And his wife would soon be turning thirty.

Cressida seemed to have been constructed from the same material as Olivia and the Bodkin-Brown wives only with a little added lumber, placed strategically where it was most likely to be noticed by anyone blessed with eyesight.

Agatha was unable to catch Betty's eye which was just as well as she may have burst out laughing. As it transpired Betty was doing her utmost to catch Simpson's eye lest it stray in a direction that she deemed out of bounds. There would be a penalty to pay in such a situation that would be more severe than stroke and distance. Thankfully, Simpson kept his drive straight, so to speak, and avoided any hint of inappropriate gaping.

'Sorry we were a bit late. I was chairing a meeting at the cricket club. Finances. Awfully dull. Much prefer playing.'

'I do, too, sir,' said Simpson. 'I used to open for my regiment. Lady Elizbeth, on the other hand is more of a golfer.'

Burnham regarded Betty for a moment, 'Well you must come down to us sometime. We have a new course just opened. Nine holes at the moment but we hope to make an eighteen one day.'

With such a good start to the proceedings, it was little surprise that the dinner proved to be an excellent evening. Burnham was a more entertaining conversationalist than any man with a wife half his age had a right to be. He was sat beside Agatha while Betty placed herself, contrary to dinner table etiquette, between Simpson and the second Lady Burnham. Simpson was at the other end of the table away from temptation and chatted happily with Olivia.

'What brings you to this part of the world?' asked Burnham after fielding a few questions on his studies from Agatha.

Agatha sensed a slight hush in the room when she answered.

'Well, aside from seeing our wonderful friends again, we're here to see the village Hallowe'en festival on Tuesday.'

Betty, less aware of the room temperature, piped up, 'And we're helping James investigate a couple of deaths that occurred in the region over the last week or two.'

'I say, how exciting,' said Burnham, clearly unfazed by the idea that women could play an equal and active part in such an investigation. Agatha noted this with some satisfaction and no little wonder.

'I imagine you might be surprised at women helping the police force in such a matter,' suggested Agatha with a smile.

'Why?' barked Burnham although not in an angry way. 'Of course, they should. Damn fools in the police would be better for it in my book. Lots of things they could do. Damn sight more observant for a start. Why Cressida can spot my faults at fifty paces. What?'

Everyone laughed and discussion moved away from the case towards something less controversial. Apparently, women's suffrage qualified in this criteria. Burnham's views on this chimed with the rest of the room.

'It's a shame that in 1876, a woman can neither vote nor control her own fortune. I suspect the two are linked, what?'

Agatha was almost clapping by this stage. Interestingly Nobby was also proving to be something of a brick in this regard.

'Quite right Burnham. Look at Olivia and me. You don't need to be a genius to see who has the brains in this relationship,' said Nobby looking at his wife affectionately.

'While you have all the looks, Nobby,' joked Simpson.
Olivia had the grace to laugh at this as it was so palpably untrue. Betty seemed less amused by the joke but smiled gamely all the same. The food kept flowing to the table like waves to a beach on a blustery day. Mulligatawny soup, Fricandeau of Veal with Spinach, steamed pudding, cheesecakes.

Agatha gave up after the veal, but Betty ploughed on before thinking better of the cheesecake. Best not to risk over-indulgence in a room full of women who were quite as striking as the wives of the two noblemen. Might give Simpson ideas. Ideas in men were not good. They led to actions that were not always in their interests, which is to say, a woman's interests.

'Can we not tempt you with cheesecake?' asked Olivia to Agatha.

The truthful answer was that Agatha felt that such extravagance would have to wait until after she was married. This was an acknowledgement that, notwithstanding her views on the rights of women, some things remained immutable. Even Betty had had to restrain her natural instincts in this regard. Part of Agatha felt an anger that she had to play the game in this manner. But there was a vanity there, too. She wanted to be noticed. Desired, even. These thoughts raced through her mind as she looked at Olivia. To say any of them would have given offence, potentially.

'It was a wonderfully large helping of veal. I think it's the best I've ever tasted.'

It had been. There were murmurs of assent and appreciation for the cook around the room.

'I shall tell cook,' said Nobby, meaning that Olivia would probably be the one to remember to do so. He was on his second bottle of wine, after all.

Conversation broke off into smaller groups as more drinks were served. Agatha chatted happily with Burnham and asked him more about his medieval studies. Hoping that the others would be too engaged in their own conversations, she risked a little bit more.

'Have you looked at much witchcraft?

Burnham grinned broadly and Agatha knew she'd hit the bull's eye. It was clear this was a subject that he was as knowledgeable about as he was passionate.

'Oh yes, my dear. It's a fascinating topic. A thread right through our history, in fact.'

'Really?' asked Agatha leaning forward.

'Yes, of course there are fewer witches now. Fewer tribes left.'

'Tribes?' said Agatha.

'Oh, indeed my dear. A bit like a cricket team. You have batsmen and bowlers. Of course, over the centuries the tribes mixed up, but you can still see the differences.'

'What types of witches are there?'

'Well, some are more skilled at those things we traditionally associate with witches. Potions and spells and the like. In reality, they are neither. I would characterise them more as medical practitioners, closer to a doctor than a nurse, certainly.'

'And the others?'

'The others have more esoteric skills. For example, mediums, divination one sees at fairgrounds have their roots in witchcraft. So, too, Astral projection.'

Agatha looked bemused at this term. Burnham smiled and explained further.

'This is perhaps the most interesting area for me. There are many women who have claimed the ability to have an out of the body experience. Of course, implicit in this idea is the idea of the soul. That we are more than just the physical manifestation we see before us. I certainly hope I am anyway,' laughed Burnham.

Agatha laughed, too, but it soon died on her lips as she realised that the rest of the table was listening to the conversation.

'I think you do yourself a disservice, sir. How do you manage to stay so fit?' asked Agatha playfully.

This gave Burnham the opportunity to talk about the other great passion in his life, cricket. The rest of the table returned to talking as if, somehow, cricket could be less interesting than witchcraft.

The end of the evening came all too soon. Burnham and his wife departed just before midnight. All agreed that they were a charming couple. Agatha, however, sensed Olivia's eyes on her. Furthermore, she suspected that Olivia was desirous to talk with her. Rather than have the broom hanging over her head, so to speak, she decided to make straight for Nobby's wife.

'I must say, I've had a very entertaining evening, Olivia.'

'Yes, I'm sorry Burnham couldn't come before but he is a charmer.'

'Clearly,' laughed Agatha, one eyebrow arched.

'Indeed,' smiled Olivia. 'We were so glad he found someone again after losing Luna. Alas, some illnesses are beyond even witchcraft.'

There it was. No allusion. No insulation. Just a direct reference. To one side Betty was bidding good night to Nobby so Agatha and Olivia went over to join the others.

'I'm off to bed, too, my darling,' said Nobby. 'Are you coming?'

'No, Agatha and I want to have a chat, my love. You know us ladies,' said Olivia. Nobby clearly did and exited stage left pretty sharpish along with Simpson who followed Betty up the stairs, eyes fixed on her lower half which, to Agatha's eyes, was moving in a way she hadn't seen before.

There was something in the air about this part of England clearly.

*

The two ladies retired to the library for a brandy. At least Agatha partook. Olivia stayed with water. Agatha had noticed she'd barely touched alcohol all evening.

'Are congratulations in order?' asked Agatha, smiling.

Olivia smiled but her eyes also began to well up. Her hand went instinctively to her stomach.

'We hope so. It's still very early days. In May.'

The Witchfinder General Murders

Agatha gave Olivia a gentle hug and professed herself delighted by the news. She sat down again, and the two ladies regarded one another for a few moments.

'You seemed to enjoy the company of Lord Burnham immensely. I'm glad. I like him very much,' said Olivia with a low opening bid.

'Yes. Unusually broad-minded for a man. But then Nobby seems to be so, too. Always has been,' replied Agatha, still keeping her cards close to her chest.

'But what do you make of all this talk of witches? I mean in this day and age,' said Oliva in a dismissive tone that was unlikely to fool anyone save for Simpson.

'Scarcely seems credible, I agree,' said Agatha.

'Yet I think you believe him, Agatha. How does all this relate to the death of Mrs Carr?'

Olivia fixed her eyes on Agatha and the smile faded a little. This was a very different woman to the one Agatha thought Nobby had married. There was a depth she'd not seen before. This depth was in feeling as well as intellect. Agatha's view of Olivia had changed enormously over the course of the two trips to Holbrigg Hall. She was proving a more formidable woman than first appearances had suggested. Agatha liked her the better for it. It was clear that Olivia was either tired or merely tired of jockeying for position. Agatha rather agreed, it seemed pointless to remain cautious. Both knew what the subject was.

'I can't be certain, but it certainly relates to the death of Mr Larwood.'

Olivia's face was already naturally pale or, at least, appeared so against the lustrous blue-black hair. For a moment it grew paler.

'Go on.'

'Without more evidence, I don't want to say that Ophelia Carr and Mr Larwood were connected. But we are alone, Olivia and I know this conversation will not be disclosed beyond ourselves and Nobby.'

Olivia nodded.

'I believe Larwood may have been, in some way, responsible for Ophelia Carr's death. I don't know that he killed her, however. It's only a hypothesis.'

Agatha paused to see if there was any hint of confirmation from Olivia. Instead, Olivia asked the obvious question.

'Why do you believe they are connected?'

'Because three years ago Mrs Carr and Mrs Dahlia went to the British Library to find books on witchcraft. That one act alerted Larwood.'

Olivia looked shocked by this. She set her glass of water down. Tears formed in her eyes.

'How?' she asked, her voice barely audible.

'The librarian in the British Library was asked by the police to inform them of any interest in books related to witchcraft. Of course, it wasn't the police. It was Larwood pretending to be a detective.'

'So, the library has been informing Larwood of anyone who requested books on witchcraft,' said Olivia. Her eyes were burning not just with tears now. The anger in her voice palpable.

'Olivia, they didn't know. The librarian in question was blameless. He thought it was the police he was communicating with.'

Olivia looked away and tried to collect herself. The urgency in Agatha's voice had surprised her and the anger evaporated as quickly as it had come. She had revealed too much of herself, she knew. How had Agatha divined all this? Could there be another explanation? She looked at Lady Agatha closely.

'How did you find all of this out?'

Agatha related the whole story of her trip to the British Library and meeting with Sir Anthony Panizzi. Olivia's remained silent but Agatha had an overwhelming sense of her personality, her emotions and her mind listening to what she was saying. When Agatha finished Olivia asked the next obvious question.

'But you've told the Library to stop now?'

'No,' replied Agatha. 'Of course not.'

Olivia gripped the arm of her chair and she leaned forward, eyes ablaze.

'But why...?' Olivia stopped mid-sentence and then she sat back and looked away. A smile appeared on her face and she turned to Agatha with something that only afterwards she realised was admiration.

'How clever, Agatha. If someone else comes along and makes the same request...'

'Correct,' responded Agatha.

Olivia shook her head and smiled at the simplicity of it. Then she fixed her eyes on Agatha and said, 'I've always admired you, Agatha. You are, that is to say, I thought once...' Then she stopped herself.

'That I was one of you?' asked Agatha, a smile appearing on her face, too.

Olivia laughed. It was a laugh that was as genuine as it was embarrassed.

'What do you think I am, Agatha?'

Agatha thought for a moment and then replied, 'A continuation of a tradition in Nobby's case; a descendant of a special community.'

Olivia held up her glass of water in acknowledgement to Agatha.

'I think witch is such a misunderstood word, don't you? It's 1876, after all. The very idea,' laughed Olivia. Then she continued, 'Once upon a time you might have been considered one of us. For all I know you may be, Agatha. I haven't decided yet. Burnham was right. We come in many shapes and sizes and colours and skills.'

There was silence for a few moments. Olivia once more seemed to be grappling with strong emotions. Agatha could sense her disquiet and remained silent. Olivia's eyes were moist once more and even Agatha could feel herself becoming emotional.

'Will you catch the men who did this to Ophelia?'

Agatha found herself unable to breathe for a moment then she replied in a whisper, 'Yes, Olivia. But this time they must face justice.'

She'd said, this time, thought Olivia. Silence returned for a few moments as Olivia considered Agatha. There was no hiding the genuine wonder in her eyes. You could be, thought Olivia. You could be.

Agatha, meanwhile, found her mind spinning from the conversation. A thought had taken root, just moments before, that was so overpowering, it had taken her breath away.

Olivia had said *men.*

This meant three things to Agatha. Larwood had been involved in Ophelia Carr's death. Of this she was certain. Furthermore, her dream was proving to be unerringly accurate.

Agatha did not want to think about the implications of this notwithstanding the insinuation from Olivia. And then there was what Olivia appeared to know. She had all but confirmed Larwood and at least two other men had committed the murder. Either she had had a similar vision or dream or...

Or she knew where Evelyn Carr was.

The room fell silent for a moment that stretched into seconds. The two women lost in their thoughts. Finally, Agatha spoke again. There was urgency in her voice.

'Olivia, I repeat. Where is Evelyn Carr? You must tell me where she is.'

Olivia shook her head. Uncertainty clouded her face. Agatha remained silent. The firelight caused shadows to dance on the walls of the room.

'I can't tell you. I don't understand why you need to know, Agatha. She's safe. That's all that matters.'

Agatha sat forward and put her glass down on the table. Olivia was surprised by the intensity in her eyes. There was worry there too if she was not mistaken. She was sure that Agatha was holding something back. In fact, Olivia was certain of this. Without knowing everything on Agatha's mind there could be no sharing of secrets.

'She can never be safe, Olivia. Never. As long as these vile men exist, she will have to live in fear. In hiding. You know this. You and those who are shielding her. Help me, Olivia. Help me stop them. It was Nobby, wasn't it, who alerted Scotland Yard? He told your MP. Your MP contacted the Commissioner. You went to a lot of trouble to have the police involved. You wanted help. Please let us help you. Let me give you one more reason why you should. Another lady who was uncovered by Larwood at the British Library, Celeste Caradoc was found hanging in her house a week after her visit to the Library. These men are dangerous, and they clearly stop at nothing.'

Olivia stood up from her seat and walked to the window. Her hand rested on the back an armchair. Agatha could see her grip tighten. There was nothing else that Agatha could say now. It was for Olivia to decide. Outside the darkness was illuminated by a moon that would soon be full.

'I cannot,' said Olivia turning back to Agatha. Her voice was almost pleading. 'It's not for me to say. You understand that don't you?'

Agatha sat back in her chair. She'd expected this answer. What else could Olivia say? It was asking too much from her. She had been trusted by Evelyn and her protector to keep her secret. To betray it on what amounted to a wager was more than could be expected. Why should she reveal such a secret when Agatha had not revealed hers?

'I understand, Olivia. But please, I urge you. Send Evelyn and the person who is shielding her a message from me. Between us we can find the murderers. We have a chance.'

Olivia walked over and sat down beside Agatha again.

'Very well. I will send the message. A rider will be despatched tomorrow morning. Tell me what you want to do.'

20

Holbrigg Hal, Norfolk: 30th October 1876

After breakfast, the next morning Agatha and Betty took a stroll with Talleyrand. Upon their return they made ready for the carriage ride to Bury St Edmunds. An inquiry if the hound would like to accompany them was swiftly dismissed as he trotted off in search of his newfound friends.

Agatha, Betty and Simpson set off for Bury St Edmunds. The conversation in the carriage was remarkably restrained given the heady ingredients provided by the previous evening. In fact, had Agatha not been pondering why things were so mutedly polite she would have noticed a certain sheepishness in the manner of her two friends.

As neither seemed up to discussing the case then Agatha decided not to share her thoughts from the conversation with Olivia. Instead, the carriage reached Bury St Edmunds and the house of the deceased Mr Larwood without any discussion never mind agreement as to what they were going to look for.

Waiting at the house was Constable Royston Elms. If he was surprised by the presence of the women, he certainly did little to disguise it. His mouth dropped open as Simpson introduced Agatha and then Betty as his colleagues. At Agatha's request he'd dropped their titles. She felt it was quite enough for the poor man to take in the presence of women; the addition of their titles might have tipped him over the edge of a precipice.

Instead, Agatha was able to enjoy the spectacle of the poor constable trying to deal with the extraordinary question of who was in charge. He resolved it by addressing his comments to a space somewhere between Agatha and Simpson. Agatha was oddly impressed by the solution.

All of Larwood's papers remained at the police station. This would give them a chance to see what letters had been sent from the British Library. Instead, Agatha was left by the others to wander around the house. She tried to develop a mental picture of everything that she saw. Was everything there that was meant to be there? What was missing? This was every bit as important in Agatha's view.

She'd tried to explain as they walked from the carriage that her friends should search without searching. This had probably been registered by Betty, but such an instruction was always likely to be lost on Simpson. By avoiding having a fixed idea on what you were looking for you would retain an open mind on everything that you did find.

The house was small and well ordered. One did not need to be a detective to see that it was very male. There was a lack of ornamentation, no extraneous furnishing. This was a man who lived alone, who was happy to be alone and who foresaw no reason or need to alter this happy situation. And then Agatha realised what was missing.

The presence of a woman.

Agatha had not seen a photograph of Larwood. There were no pictures in the house. However, she understood from Simpson that he'd been considered a fine looking rather than handsome gentleman. She wondered why he would have chosen to remain single given his obvious appeal as a man of relative means.

They left the house after half an hour and went to the police station to look through his personal affects. The papers had remained there following the open verdict from Colonel Magilton. No one had come to claim them, which was another point of interest to Agatha.

'There are relatives?'

'Yes, but they live in the north of the country. A brother and the deceased's nephews,' confirmed Elms he handed over a large box to Simpson. He led the group to a police prison cell as there were no other rooms that they could use to examine the documents. Agatha looked around at the forbidding grey walls.

'Aunt Daphne thinks I'll end up in one of these places someday. I must tell her that her prediction came true.'

'Wish rather than prediction, you mean,' laughed Betty.

'This will be my punishment for not getting married,' agreed Agatha.

'A different type of life sentence,' whispered Betty as Simpson moved out of ear shot.

They split the documents into three piles. Betty and Simpson dealt with personal correspondence while Agatha took the larger chits and receipts that Larwood had retained. Elms looked in on them from time to time.

'Constable Elms,' asked Agatha at one point, 'Who else has looked through these documents?'

'Only Colonel Magilton and I.'

'What was the Colonel looking for?'

'He was mostly interested in the financial affairs of Mr Larwood. He ignored the other papers for the most part and asked me if I'd seen anything that might have given a clue to his state of mind.'

'Did he say what he meant by that?'

'Yes. Any disagreements with his family or letters which suggested he was involved romantically.

Agatha nodded. Magilton was no fool even if he was insufferable. By this stage Agatha had been through most of the financial papers that Larwood had kept.

'There are no obvious financial troubles as far as I can see,' announced Agatha to the others.

'That was Colonel Magilton's conclusion, too, ma'am,' added Elms.

'Why do you think this important, Agatha?' asked Simpson.

'I think the colonel, like me, wanted to find a motive for suicide. Now as far as we are aware, Larwood had few friends, had never been linked with anyone romantically. His work colleagues said that he was a serious-minded but fair man, not subject to any signs of volatility. Is this correct, Constable Elms?'

'Yes,' replied Elms. His attention was now fully on Agatha. She was clearly the senior officer. What wonders this modern age was providing. A woman police officer who sounded as if she was from the nobility. Meanwhile Agatha continued, as much for her own benefit as the others.

'Then the only other obvious motive I can think of is financial. Colonel Magilton, quite correctly in my view, wanted to exclude that from any motive for suicide. From what I can see, and I am no professional, but his affairs look in order. He was a wealthy man. Of course, we can never know what goes on inside anyone's mind. Feelings such as anger and hatred as well as love and fear can be hidden away. But unless you have seen something of a personal nature crop up in the letters that you went through then I agree with Colonel Magilton. There was no obvious reason that Larwood should commit suicide never mind in the awful manner that he did.'

'But is he not being inconsistent?' asked Betty. 'Why does he question the death of Larwood and not Ophelia Carr?'

'The evidence. It's basic algebra.'

Betty frowned at her friend.

'I was always terrible at that beastly subject as you well know, Agatha. So, trust me when I say, I have no earthly idea what you mean.'

Simpson and Elms were both relieved that Betty had said this for they hadn't much idea either. Agatha took a deep breath thereby further giving the indication that she was speaking to recalcitrant school children.

'Colonel Magilton has been completely consistent. In one case there is evidence, at least highly suggestive evidence, of suicide. In the second case, we have the other side of the equation, a suicide without anything to suggest why this man would have done what he did. Even if you question the motives in the first case, and I do, there's no question Colonel Magilton was merely taking the path of least resistance. There was a letter. There is nothing here. I think the colonel, as much as I hate to admit this for, I found him unbearably smug, has acted correctly.'

This mollified the others but was hardly satisfactory. The need for evidence in criminal cases was a dashed nuisance sometimes when one could just *feel* the solution.

'So, what do we do now?' asked Betty.

'Enjoy the festival tomorrow. Unless we can show that something similar has happened, then we have nothing further we can do here. For example, have there been any similar cases in the area, Constable Elms?'

Elms' eyes widened at the question. His respect for Scotland Yard's recruitment policy was now at an all-time high.

'There was.'

All eyes turned to Constable Elms. The elderly constable reddened a little at the attention or perhaps it was the realisation that perhaps he should have mentioned this before now. Agatha spoke first. Her voice was gentle and soft. This was as dangerous as Agatha could get. It signalled an eruption was not very far away.

'There was a similar case to this?'

'Yes ma'am.'

'When?'

'A long time ago,' said Elms with a little bit of relief. Perhaps the passing of time would make it less relevant.

'Go on,' pressed Agatha. Betty could almost see ash falling like raindrops in the room.

'Well, as I say it was a long time ago. At least twenty years. A man, not unlike Mr Larwood, a single man who was in his middle age committed, what appeared to be suicide, in the middle of a village.'

'With a knife?' asked Betty.

'No, he hanged himself from a tree. No one tried to stop him. They didn't notice what he was doing until it was too late.'

'You say it wasn't in Bury St Edmunds?'

'No, this happened just outside Ipswich, but I remember reading about it. The verdict was left open as no suicide note was found and nothing could explain why he'd done it.'

Agatha looked thoughtfully at Elms.

'Did you mention the case to Colonel Magilton?'

'Yes, I did mention it, in fact,' said Elms in a manner of someone trying to show that he was not a complete dolt. Agatha's eyes narrowed a little at this.

'Did he ask you to find out more about the verdict from the inquest?'

'As a matter of fact, he did,' responded Elms.

Agatha breathed slowly. It felt like she was pulling teeth.

'The verdict, constable?'

Elms reddened a little and replied, ''Open.'

'Well now we know why the colonel went with the open verdict,' said Simpson.

'There was precedent,' agreed Betty.

The group stood up at this point. They had found out all they needed for the moment. Elms accompanied them to the entrance of the police station, and they bid farewell. The carriage was waiting for them and they climbed in. Just as they were about to leave Agatha used her ever-present umbrella to hit the roof of the cab. The cab stopped immediately.

'I forgot. There's one more thing I need to ask Constable Elms.'

Betty was about to ask Agatha what that might be when she realised that for the next minute or two, she had James Simpson all to herself in a carriage. Simpson was of a similar mind.

It must be said that when Elms saw Agatha return his heart sank somewhat. He'd had quite enough excitement for one day. A little bit of this remarkable lady went quite a long way.

'Constable Elms, I do have one more question.'

You would, thought Elms.

'The other death, twenty years ago. Was there a case of a woman dying or committing suicide sometime before it? A death in similarly strange circumstances?'

Elms looked at Agatha in shock. Agatha didn't need to hear his answer. It was written all over the constable's face. The implications were enormous, but she shouldn't be hasty. It would be too easy to jump to conclusions.

'Thank you, constable, I can see by your face there was. Just before you tell me what happened, I have another question.'

A few minutes later when Agatha returned, she found the two sweethearts sitting opposite one another looking innocently out the window. It was immediately apparent that neither had missed her in the intervening minutes. The carriage set off to Nobby's mansion. Agatha had much food for thought.

21

Holbrigg Hall, Norfolk: 31ˢᵗ October 1876

The party set off soon after lunch to attend the Hallowe'en festival at Upper Outwell. The heatless sunshine meant everyone was well wrapped up with thick coats and mittens. The countryside was a crystal kingdom. Frost sparkled on the dead sticks in the grass. The lake near the mansion was beginning to freeze. The wheels of the carriage crunched over the hard frosty ground. On the way, Nobby told them a little bit more about the festival.

'As you know, a village year revolves around festivals. Most are church-related. This one is something of a meeting point between pagan and Christianity. The harvest season is over and we're entering the darker half of the year. It all dates back to the early days of the village.'

'I gather when the village was first founded by the Saxons, they had a festival of fertility in late October whereby villagers and farmers from the area would offer a sacrifice, not human I would add, so that the crops would grow the following spring and summer. Then there would be the usual harvest festival in September. We celebrate fertility quite frequently, it seems.' added Nobby with a chortle.

Olivia raised one eyebrow by way of admonishment. However, the impact of the gentle rebuke was undermined by the fact that her hand was on her stomach and she'd revealed, the previous evening, that she and Nobby were going to have a baby.

The journey was quicker than before because the wheels were skipping over the icy ground. When they arrived at the village the visitors declared themselves impressed by what they saw.

The village had been transformed over the course of the week. The green was dotted with stalls which circled the large wooden frame. One might kindly have described it as a figure. It would have required a stretch of the imagination to say that the figure was the Prince of Darkness. They would set the figure alight towards the end of the festivities symbolically providing warmth and sustenance in the cold night air. Agatha found the idea odd in the extreme. Although she hadn't confessed this even to her friends, she disliked the village intensely. There was an atmosphere about the place at once unwelcoming and strange.

A crowd of villagers were trooping towards the green: farmers, labourers and their families, children all dressed in Sunday best. Outside the church, the tall figure of Reverend Lumley stood at the entrance saying hello to the villagers. He smiled benignly at Agatha and the others as they alighted from the carriage. Another large carriage sat near the entrance to the church. Agatha turned to Nobby and asked who it belonged to.

'Oh, that's Raymond Du Maurier, he owns a lot of land to the west. We usually see him at these things. Doesn't really appear much at church, though. Not sure he believes in much aside from making pots of money.'

The Witchfinder General Murders

'Which one is he?'

Nobby had a look around and then spotted the man in question.

'That's him over there near young Dr Wilson.'

Agatha scanned the crowd and then she saw the two men. Her mouth dropped open.

'Good lord,' said Agatha.

She glanced at Nobby and Olivia who were both looking at her with half smiles.

She looked again at the two men and then back to her hosts. Neither seemed prepared to say anything so Agatha did.

'There's quite a close resemblance,' said Agatha, dipping her toe more delicately than normal into the murky waters of tittle-tattle.

'Do you think so?' asked Olivia a little too innocently.

Do I ever? Thought Agatha. They were all too clearly father and son. Raymond du Maurier was in his forties with dark curly hair, greying at the sides. He was as tall as Dr Wilson; his eyes were clear and dangerous looking. Dangerous, that is, if you were a female. He was decidedly every bit as good-looking as the young doctor. He wore a long light brown coat, and breeches that clung to a very muscular leg if Agatha's eyes did not deceive her. Agatha shot Olivia a look but decided against answering as her reaction had made more than plain what her view was.

'Strange cove,' said Nobby. 'Employs a lot of the village on his farm but he doesn't really take much to do with the management. More of a businessman than a farmer. Obviously works, though. Owns a big place on the road to Hunstanton. I've never been but apparently, he owns a townhouse in London and one in the south of France. Doesn't take much to do with us. He has business interests in London. Export and whatnot.'

As Agatha was pondering the relationship between the doctor and the wealthy landowner, matters became even more strange when Dr Wilson senior walked over with Mrs Wilson. The only thing that the diminutive older doctor and the younger one, in Agatha's view, had in common was their profession and their name.

Olivia took Agatha's arm and said, 'Shall I introduce you?'

Agatha looked at Olivia archly, 'Are you sure you can trust me, Olivia?'

Olivia burst out laughing at this and they walked forward. The younger Dr Wilson spotted the arrival of Agatha and gently nudged du Maurier. He looked up and regarded the two ladies in a manner that Agatha interpreted as appraisal.

'Mr du Maurier, what a pleasure to see you again,' said Olivia. The greeting was friendly-formal, as if she were trying to make it seem that they did not see one another very often. Dr Wilson and du Maurier both bowed to the two ladies.

'Countess Olivia, the pleasure is all mine,' said du Maurier nobly. His voice was deep, rich and seductive. He took Olivia's hand and kissed it. Then he turned his attention to Agatha.

'And this must be the Lady Agatha I've been hearing so much about.'

'I'm on my guard, sir, be warned,' responded Agatha. 'Do I have to live up or down to what you've heard?'

'You've already exceeded all expectations, my lady. Dr Wilson has told me what an impressive mind you possess.'

Agatha glanced at Wilson and smiled. The good doctor's smile was a replica of the landowner's.

'Dr Wilson is very gallant.'

'Are you and Mr Simpson still investigating the death of Mrs Carr?' asked Wilson. 'I noticed you left before Colonel Magilton gave his verdict. There were no surprises, I'm afraid.'

'So, I understand,' replied Agatha. 'He seemed more suspicious about a death in Bury St Edmonds, however. Have you heard about it?'

'Yes, strange case. Another suicide,' said Wilson, nodding. There was no disguising the disdain in his voice. 'I hadn't realised Magilton was the magistrate. It was an open finding, wasn't it?'

The older Dr Wilson broke in at this point, 'It seems a shame to be talking about such matters, my boy. Think of your mother.'

'I quite agree,' piped up Mrs Wilson. This effectively ended the conversation much to the irritation of young Dr Wilson. The face of du Maurier was one of benign amusement. At this point Betty arrived with Simpson and Nobby in tow. One look at Betty's face told Agatha that she'd picked up on the relationship between Wilson and du Maurier. Simpson seemed oblivious.

'Hello du Maurier, do you fancy getting this show started?' asked Nobby shaking hands with the big landowner.

'No Manningfield, I will leave that in your capable hands,' laughed du Maurier. It was not said unkindly and Nobby laughed along with him. There was clearly little by way of rivalry between the two main landowners in the area and even some warmth.

Reverend Lumley had now joined the group. He looked at Nobby with raised eyebrows and said, 'Shall we?'

Nobby took Olivia's arm and walked towards a small, wooded platform that had been erected in front of the bonfire.

At the sight of the three people walking into the centre, the rest of the villagers and visitors from the surrounding area piled onto the green and followed them towards the platform.

A few minutes later with around two hundred people grouped around the platform, Lumley led the audience in a prayer for the dead. When it was finished, he turned to Nobby and asked him to declare the Hallowe'en Festival open.

Nobby smiled and gripped the lapels of his coat in the manner of a man about to deliver a long speech. Agatha sincerely hoped that this would not be the case. Thankfully, she and her friend were of a like mind.

'I think you know me by now,' started Nobby. There was a ripple of sympathetic laughter. 'Hallowe'en is celebrated in many places, but I believe few celebrate it as well or as enthusiastically as the village of Upper Outwell.'

This brought cheers from all assembled.

'I think the children are impatient to see the Punch and Judy show, bob for apples and whatnot. The wonderful news for the Countess and myself is that we will soon have one of our own children joining you in the fun.'

This brought a loud cheer from the assembly. Just as Nobby was about to speak again, du Maurier shouted out, 'Three cheers for the Earl and the Countess.'

He led the cheering and when they had finished, Nobby thanked him and duly declared the festival open. All of a sudden, the stalls were surrounded by men, women children.

Agatha found Dr Wilson's taking her arm and leading her over towards the Punch and Judy show. It was proving to be a popular destination for the children.

166

'I'm surprised you would approve of such an entertainment,' said Wilson with a smile.

'I don't. I'm hoping that it might have a more commendable plot than the one I grew up watching.'

'You might be surprised by this version,' said Wilson enigmatically. As he said this, Agatha's attention was attracted by two farm labourers. They were tall, well made and both could have been related to Dr Wilson and Mr du Maurier. Thankfully Wilson had not seen what had caught her attention. The show was about to start as indicated by the growing hum of excitement from the children.

A lute began to play a haunting but beautiful melody from behind the stall. Agatha was entranced. The curtain drew back and onto the stage marched Punch. The character spoke in the traditional squawked voice. He was chatting about the Hallowe'en when all of a sudden, another character appeared. This character was a devil-like character. Punch began to panic, running backwards and forwards. The devil grabbed a hold of Punch and proclaimed his intention of dragging him into the flames of hell.

'Rather strong,' whispered Agatha to Wilson.

The doctor laughed and pointed to the audience of children, all under the age of ten who appeared to be baying for blood. Then rescue was at hand. Judy appeared bringing cheers from the audience. But this was one was like no Judy Agatha had ever seen before. She was dressed in black and appeared to be travelling on a broomstick and clutching a magic wand. It would have been quite something if this extraordinary spectacle had finished with some manner of magic. However, the witch was schooled in the art and, it must be said, tropes of the genre. She proceeded to batter, quite literally, the hell out of the devil,

167

sending him packing to the cheers of the audience and the gratitude of the rather passive Punch.

The show finished and the two puppeteers made an appearance in front of the stage. This was the second shock of the early afternoon. They were both women. One was Beatrix Dahlia and the other was her friend that Agatha had often seen her with. She turned to Dr Wilson who was regarding her with amusement.

'I must confess, I didn't anticipate any of what I've just witnessed.'

'Does this meet with your approval?', said Wilson, grinning broadly.

'With some qualification, yes,' laughed Agatha.

They walked away from the Punch and Judy performers towards another platform that was proving jolly good fun for the kids if not a little bizarre. They were throwing cream pies at a man in makeshift wooden stocks. Agatha looked from the cream-covered face of the man to Wilson for an explanation.

'A useful method of learning history?' asked the embarrassed Wilson. Agatha laughed but shook her head, too.

'Stranger and stranger, Dr Wilson.' She looked at the man who was bent forward with his head and arm placed inside holes for the children to aim at. Despite the cream there was something familiar about him. When the children ran out of cream pies, the man was released from his captivity. He was given a towel to wipe the cream from his face and hands. 'Good Lord, isn't that the young man who is mentally incapable?'

'Ned? Whatever made you think him mentally incapable?'

'But I thought you said?' replied Agatha.

'No, I meant his was a sad story. He lost his parents when he was sixteen. He's had to fend for himself. He's as bright as you or me but he's always been a troubled boy.'

They moved on to view the next stall. Further ahead there was the sound of cockerels. Lots of them. Some men were standing beside the cages housing the cockerels. Just as she was about to ask Wilson why they were in cages; Agatha heard a voice from behind her.

'Lady Agatha?'

Agatha and Wilson turned around. The voice was that of Beatrix Dahlia. She walked forward and looked at Wilson.

'Lady Agatha, may I introduce Miss Dahlia. You may have seen her at the inquest.'

'Yes, I remember. Hello Miss Dahlia.'

Beatrix Dahlia looked a little uncomfortable. She glanced at Wilson and then said, 'Lady Agatha may I ask, are you still investigating the death of Ophelia Carr?'

'I'm not officially part of the investigation, such as it is,' replied Agatha carefully.

'This was not my question, Lady Agatha. Are you investigating her death?'

A little more direct that she was used to, but Agatha was not a woman to mind such an approach. What was the point in beating around the bush?

'Yes, my friend and I are assisting Mr Simpson.'

'Would you care to come with me for a cup of tea? There's something I would like to tell you.'

Agatha glanced at Wilson who smiled and nodded. The doctor tried, and failed, to give that impression that he knew nothing of Miss Dahlia's desire to speak with her.

'Very well,' replied Agatha. At this point Betty came over having seen Agatha chatting with Miss Dahlia. Introductions were made and the two ladies followed Miss Dahlia to a beautiful, thatched cottage on the green. Ivy climbed the white walls, creating the impression of a cottage that was a living entity.

There was only one floor to the house. Agatha and Betty entered through the front door and found themselves immediately in the living area. It was small inside with a low ceiling although this was unlikely ever to trouble either Betty or Agatha. The floor was wooden and the walls where white-washed. There were a number of wooden seats and a dining table. A small fire burned in the hearth which appeared to double as the kitchen area.

'Please sit down,' said Miss Dahlia. Another woman appeared from one of the rooms. This was the second lady from the Punch and Judy show.

'This is my friend Miss Ursula Piper. Ursula, may I introduce Lady Agatha and Lady Elizabeth. They are both helping the young policeman in his inquires.'

Miss Piper smiled and offered to make the tea.

'I must congratulate you both on an unusual Punch and Judy show. Most unexpected,' smiled Agatha. She glanced down at a lute propped up against the wall. 'A beautiful melody also. Is it your own composition?'

'No,' replied Miss Piper. 'It's a traditional piece.'

'It was beautiful. Quite a contrast in tone to the performance.'

Miss Dahlia laughed and replied, 'I don't think Punch should have things all his own way.'

'Nor do I,' agreed Agatha. 'A witch, though. Very interesting.'

170

The Witchfinder General Murders

Miss Dahlia smiled and exchanged looks with her friend.

'I think that is a good point to explain my reasons for wishing to meet you. As you may have gathered from the inquest, we believe Ophelia Carr was murdered. Or to be more precise, executed without trial by men who have been performing such vile acts for centuries.'

'Good Lord,' said Betty, beating Agatha to this particular punch. 'How can this be?'

'Have you heard of a man called Matthew Hopkins?' asked Miss Dahlia.

Betty wisely waited for Agatha to confirm if they'd heard of him. She couldn't remember his name among the people mentioned at the inquest for either Miss Carr or Larwood.

'He was the last Witchfinder General, I believe,' replied Agatha.

'You are correct in identifying him as a Witchfinder General. He was not the last, however.'

22

Walsingham, Norfolk, September 1646

The rain which had been so incessant began to ease. It had been like this all week. The wind was hurling slates off the roof. He'd nearly been hit by one on his arrival into the town. No wonder the cough had returned. It would do for him, he knew. That or a knife in the middle of the night. But not the war. He'd escaped that, at least. It would be over soon, so they said. Naseby and Langport had proved decisive. Matthew Hopkins certainly hoped so. He'd been dragooned twice to fight. Twice he'd escaped and resumed his self-appointed role.

The weather had not been a deterrent. Dozens of towns folk had gathered in the square. All eyes were upon him. He was used to this. There was a time he'd enjoyed the attention, the fear, the blood lust in those same eyes. Now it felt sickening. He was about to speak when he felt his body tense up and he began to cough again.

He regained control of his breathing and addressed himself to the condemned woman who had been dragged, then carried before him. An old woman's face peered up at him from blackened eyes hidden partially by a tangle of knotted grey hair.

The magistrate glanced towards Hopkins. He looked nervous, thought Hopkins. Beside the magistrate stood John

Montgomery and his wife. They had been the chief witnesses in the trial of the old woman. Montgomery was also her landlord, thought Hopkins cynically. His hand touched the bag containing nine guineas he'd just received from the magistrate.

Hopkins turned his attention to the old woman.

'You are condemned Mistress Fairclough. Will you confess?' This no longer mattered in a legal sense. The lawyer in Hopkins recognised the issue was settled but it was always worth trying to set a seal on the finding. 'You are a witch. You serve Satan. You have been seen with his imps. You have diseased the cattle and the crops of this God-fearing family. It is proven. Will you not confess?'

The sullen resentment of the crowd had long since given way to impatience. They had come to see a hanging. What else was there to say? He sensed the keenness in the crowd was turning to exasperation at the improvised formality levied by Hopkins in these last few moments. The mood was turning uglier; blood-hunger burned in their eyes.

He turned away and gave a dismissive wave like Nero in the Colosseum. The crowd roared in approval. The money was in his pocket. There was no need to stay. John Stearne, his sometime assistant, had long since departed for the tavern or to find physical comfort.

He walked away as the crowd roared again and then hushed leaving the gallows to creak news of the execution of Margaret Fairclough. He pushed his way through the crowd to his lodgings.

A surprise lay in store at his room at the inn. John Stearne lay snoring on the bed. Hopkins had expected him to have company. Sitting on a chair, however, beside Hopkins' bed was a young man. He'd seen him before.

Without preamble and without standing up the young man said, 'I want to join you.'

Hopkins was weary and wanted only to sleep. He resisted the urge to hawk up half his gut.

'I've seen you before, have I not?' asked Hopkins studying the young man.

'I don't know.'

'Yes, you were at Fakenham,' replied Hopkins. There was an edge to his voice. A hint of contempt. 'Why do you wish to join us?'

'To do the Lord's work. To rid England of damnable practices.'

Hopkins sat down on a bed still dishevelled from the morning. Outside his window carts, rolled past, men and women argued in the streets. How he wanted away from this. He wanted to retire from the life and set up as a lawyer. The money he had made was more than sufficient to set himself up as a gentleman. Why wait?

He looked at the young man. He was under thirty. Why was he here? To avoid the war, probably. To make money, certainly.

'I have all I need,' said Hopkins glancing at the unconscious Stearne in the bed.

The young man smirked. Even Hopkins felt he was being ridiculous. But was he? Hopkins was the lawyer. He had the educated tongue. Stearne was a thug. His torturer-in-chief. Neither Hopkins nor Stearne were under any illusion about what they did.

'I have no use for you, begone,' said Hopkins turning away from the man.

'I can help you,' persisted the young man.

174

The Witchfinder General Murders

'Why?' Is it money you seek? Have you run away from the army? Or is it something else?' Hopkins spun around suddenly and stared into the young man's eyes. Then he smiled and nodded, 'Yes, perhaps it's something else. I can see that you have not defiled yourself. You wish to be one of the 144,000?'

Hopkins laughed mirthlessly. Then his eyes turned to flint. 'Leave me.'

*

Eight months later Hopkins' dream of living the life of a gentleman lay dying in a bed, a body wracked by coughing, a chest unable to breathe and a mind tortured by regret. But no guilt lay on the conscience of Matthew Hopkins, only anger. A lament for the time spent travelling in all weathers. His health ruined in his haste to line his pocket from rooting out witches.

Hopkins was living in a dilapidated tenement in a single room. The money earned from witch finding had dwindled as his consumption weakened his body and exhausted his energy. He lay most days looking at rats scurrying around the floor. It was the end of summer, yet he was chilled to his bones.

Callers were few so when he heard a knock at the door one evening, he thought it was a dream. The knock became more insistent.

'Go away,' he called weakly.

The door opened and a man came into the dimly lit room. Hopkins squinted to see who the visitor could be. The man's face came into focus. He recognised it vaguely but still had to ask him, 'Who are you?'

'I came to you eight months ago. I wished to join you.'

'And I refused you. You will be happy that I did so,' responded Hopkins in a tired voice.

'I still wish to serve, sir,' replied the man.

Hopkins' eyes narrowed and he waved his arm.

'Go away, I have nothing left to do but to die. Go away.'

But the young man stayed and mopped Hopkins' brow. He stayed for a week and the strength slowly returned to the former witch finder.

'What do you want?' asked Hopkins one evening as they sat at the table eating.

'I want to be like you. Like you were.'

This was greeted by laughter that turned into wracking coughs.

'Then you are mad, my boy. There is no income to be earned from witch finding now. Parliament, councils, the church all align against us. It is over.'

'But Satan and his legions will win.'

The witch finder looked at the young man. He looked at him with an intensity that the young man had not seen since he first had followed Hopkins to several trials and then executions.

'Is that what you fear?' asked Hopkins.

The young man was confused and said as much to Hopkins. This was greeted with a smile. He fixed his eyes on the young man and spoke softly.

'I don't think it is,' continued Hopkins. 'You fear sin. You fear the sin that you wish to commit. Who was she, my friend? The one who denied you. The one who chose another?'

The young man's eyes widened, and his heart began to beat like a hammer. How could he know this. He laughed nervously.

'I know not what you speak of?' said the young man thickly.

Hopkins grasped his hand.

'Yes, you do. You want revenge, don't you? I can see it in your eyes. I can see the way she has disturbed your temper. Inhabited your thoughts, your dreams. The thoughts that make

you sin so much. She is a witch. Make no mistake my friend. She is a witch.'

The young man trembled. Hopkins looked down at the young man's hand. It was shaking.

'*He will forgive you for what you've done,'* whispered Hopkins.

'*It was murder,'* cried the young man.

'*He, will forgive you, if you follow him.'*

'*Who? Who will forgive me?'*

'*The one true lord.'*

The young man frowned. His breath was coming in short bursts. He felt weak while the grip of the witch finder on his hand became stronger. He tried to remove his hand.

'*Raise your right hand,'* ordered Hopkins.

The young man was fearful now, but he did as he was told.

'*Repeat after me, sentence by sentence. I swear my allegiance...to obey without question...to give my mind, my body and my soul...to worship him...my lord Satan. I will stay true to my oath...I shall speak not of my initiation...I shall speak not of any person I have met...I shall disclose no secrets...except to those...to whom I have brought ...to the one true faith....Should I break this oath...as Satan is my witness...I shall die...a long agonising death.'*

The young man repeated the words. Hopkins released the grip on his hand.

'*You may go now.'*

177

23

When Miss Dahlia had finished there was silence in the room. Neither Miss Dahlia nor her friend spoke as they allowed the two visitors to take in what they'd heard. They understood the enormity of what they'd communicated. They accepted that it stretched credulity in an age where scientific progress was rendering the old beliefs not only redundant but ridiculous. Finally, Agatha spoke.

'How did you come by this knowledge?'

Once more the only noise to be heard inside the cottage came from the festivities outside. Miss Dahlia and Miss Piper exchanged looks and this time it was the latter who spoke.

'We are what you would call witches. Of course, this is 1876 there are no pointy hats, brooms or any of the usual iconography you might associate with this tradition.'

Just as she said this a black and white cat jumped onto the table giving Agatha a bit of start.

'Well, perhaps some,' said Miss Dahlia with a smile. 'There are hundreds, perhaps thousands of witches in the country. It is not always the case that one must be born into such a belief. Of course, this is possible, and Evelyn Carr is but one example. For others it is a choice. Witchcraft comes in many forms and not all involve magical rights. I would suggest it is more akin to ancient knowledge, beliefs and principles which have been passed down in oral and written form. Neither of us performs magic, for example, but we have a knowledge of ancient forms of healing that can provide an alternative to the methods used by doctors and vets.'

Agatha made a rapid scan of the room. It was not large. One side was given over to shelving containing small clay pots. Below, on the floor, were plants in pots which gave off a fragrance that Agatha could not identify but which she found intoxicating. There were also stacks of hemp leaves. There was no question that some form of herbalism was practiced here.

'So, you are both, forgive me for saying this, witches, but neither of you were born with any special powers. Your practice is based entirely on knowledge passed down from generation to generation.'

'That is correct Lady Agatha.'

'I say,' said Betty. 'This is extraordinary. So, you are able to provide cures for people?'

'Yes, we have helped many people with problems where standard medical practice has not succeeded.'

'Could you help me?' asked Betty.

Agatha turned sharply to Betty. What on earth was she talking about?

'Of course, my dear, what is the problem you need help with?'

'I have a slice.'

Agatha put her head in her hands and groaned.

'A slice? I'm not sure what you mean.'

Betty ignored her friend's look of censure and carried on.

'Golf. My tee shots have been careering off to the right of late. Didn't used to do that. I'm at my wits end, really.'

'We're not particularly expert on golf, my dear. I'm sorry,' said Miss Dahlia with a sympathetic smile. Betty looked very downcast, so much so that Miss Dahlia inquired a bit more about the problem.

'Well,' explained Betty, demonstrating her swing. 'I play a shot from the tee box. It starts of straight and then all of a sudden, as if by magic, it takes a sharp right and heads into trouble.'

Miss Dahlia's eyes were shut although she still managed to say, 'I see. Well, perhaps, physics can help us in this matter. If you ball turns sharply it would suggest to me that you have done something to impart spin when you make contact. Perhaps when you hit the ball your golf stick...'

'Club,' interjected Betty.

'Club, is coming across the ball.'

Miss Dahlia then proceeded to demonstrate what she meant with a rudimentary golf swing. By now Agatha's mouth was all but falling open as the witch attempted to diagnose Betty's golf troubles.

'I say, that's devilishly clever of you,' said Betty. 'So, if I can avoid coming across the ball and putting spin on it then there's a good chance, I'll stop slicing the blessed thing.'

'I hope so,' smiled Miss Dahlia. 'As I say, I'm not really an expert.'

Agatha, by this stage, was becoming increasingly less amused by the side-track Betty had taken them on. All eyes turned to Agatha who gave Betty a 'have-you-finished' look. Betty shrugged by way of a response. Agatha fixed her eyes on Miss Dahlia.

'Perhaps if we can return to the main subject. I'm interested in what beliefs witches have. For example, do you believe in God?' asked Agatha.

'Do you mean, do we consort with the devil and his familiars?' replied Miss Dahlia, her eyes twinkling.

Agatha smiled at this and shook her head.

'No, I mean do you believe in a god, gods or God? I'm curious.'

'I can't speak for everyone in our tradition, of course, but I do not believe in either God, the Holy Trinity or Satan as such. There may be one unitary divine essence, but I do not accept Christian exceptionalism. Such thinking gives permission for the atrocities that have been committed against our tradition for centuries.'

Agatha nodded in agreement. This was unarguable.

'May I ask why anyone would want to kill you? In this day and age surely, there is greater latitude to believe or not believe.'

'No one wants to kill us, Lady Agatha. By that I mean, Ursula and I are not a target for anyone, but that is not necessarily the case for those who are born into this spirit.'

'Then why are these women and men endangered? Why was Ophelia Carr killed? Why is Eveline Carr in hiding from these people?' pressed Agatha.

'Why would anyone kill another person? Jealousy? Fear? Belief?'

This was not satisfactory, and Agatha was not a woman to hide her dissatisfaction.

'Please Miss Dahlia. You know of what I speak. These are generic reasons. You must know something more about the motives of these men. After all, if you've had knowledge of witchcraft passed down to you, if you understand the history of the tradition, then you must surely know why people feared you enough to wish to persecute you.'

'Ophelia was a priestess. Evelyn was beginning to show signs that she, too, had inherited this gift. It is by no means certain that all do even if they are born into this spirit. These faculties only become apparent as you grow into adulthood. It is a very trying time. The last few years for Evelyn have been very difficult as her powers became more evident. There's so much to understand. Both Ophelia and Evelyn had gifts. These skills represent a danger to those who would seek to kill them.

'Why?' asked Agatha. Her sense of frustration increasing.

'Matthew Hopkins in his book "The Discovery of Witches" constantly accuses witches of making covenant with Satan. This is not true. It is they who are doing the Devil's work.'

'No one is arguing with you that what they are doing is evil. Why are they so fearful of you?' repeated Agatha.

'No, Lady Agatha, please listen to what I am saying,' continued Miss Dahlia. 'They are the ones doing Satan's work. Their master is Satan. They have used the persecution of witches to hide their true intentions. I repeat, they worship Satan. It is not the practice and never had been for witches to consort with, follow, or worship Satan. The Witchfinders are the ones who have made a covenant with the Devil. They believe they will be granted powers, riches and everlasting life through their vile acts. They fear witches such as Ophelia and Evelyn because they have the power to identify them.'

'How?' asked Agatha.

'They are mediums. They can see things we cannot see. Witchfinders know that they possess this power, and they fear it. That is why they kill; kill in a ritual fashion. You must find the men who did this, Lady Agatha. They must face justice for what they did.'

Agatha saw the hard glint in the eyes of Miss Dahlia.

'Like Phillip Larwood?' asked Agatha.

This shocked the two ladies into silence. More than anger, there was fear, too. A secret revealed disturbs equilibrium. It sets off a ripple that can become a tidal surge.

'What do you mean?' asked Miss Dahlia, her voice barely a whisper.

'You know what I mean, Miss Dahlia. Was he one of the killers of Miss Carr?'

The face of Miss Dahlia was a mask, but Miss Piper was less able to hide her anxiety. Her hands were gripped knuckle white.

'What do you intend to do if I find the killer of Ophelia Carr? Will he be put into a hypnotic state and kill himself like Phillip Larwood?'

Miss Dahlia's face turned white and then a rage burned in her eyes. Even Betty was somewhat taken aback by what Agatha had said. Miss Dahlia stood up sharply and glared at Agatha.

'I think you should leave Lady Agatha.'

24

Agatha nodded to Betty and they both rose from their seats, walked to the door and opened it. At the door she turned to the two ladies.

'I will never be able to prove that Larwood was put into a trance any more than I will be able to link it to a similar crime twenty years ago when Giles Shrimpton killed himself a few days after the death of a lady named Helena Jadis. Whoever killed Ophelia Carr will face justice, but I will not be part of someone's revenge.'

With that Agatha spun around and stalked out followed by Betty. When they were outside, Betty trotted to get into step with Agatha.

'Would you mind telling me what that was all about? It seems to me that you all but accused Beatrix Dahlia of murder.'

Agatha stopped and turned to her friend.

'Well, that's because she or someone like her, killed Phillip Larwood. I don't know all of the facts, but I know as sure as you are standing here facing me that they suspected Larwood's complicity in the death of Ophelia Carr and they made him kill himself. It's fantastical I know but I can see no other explanation. When I went back to see Constable Elms, I asked him if something like this had happened before and it had. A pair of similar deaths occurred twenty years ago near Ipswich.

The Witchfinder General Murders

Based on what Beatrix Dahlia has told us, I think we have an explanation of sorts about why these deaths occurred. Proving them is quite another matter.'

'Good Lord,' said Betty. If this was Agatha's hypothesis then it was as good as fact in Betty's book. 'I hope they don't turn us into frogs, Agatha. I, for one, will be severely displeased with you.'

Agatha stopped and stared at her friend.

'Granted,' continued Betty, reddening slightly, 'That is highly unlikely, but I thought I'd mention it, dear. Anyway, let's find James and tell him what we've found out.'

Before they could do so they were intercepted by Joseph Parr and his wife Amy. He raised his hat while his wife curtsied.

'Good day Lady Agatha, Lady Elizabeth. I hope you are enjoying the festival,' said Parr.

Both ladies replied that they were but added nothing more. They were eager to get away.

'I hope you will stay for the bonfire, but I must warn you it gets rather chilly by the time they set it alight.'

'I'm sure the fire will warm us up,' smiled Agatha. This signalled the end of the conversation and they moved off in search of the young policeman.

Simpson was standing beside a young woman chatting happily away when he saw Betty and Agatha approach. The warm smile fell away when he saw Betty's face. What, to him, had been an inoffensive conversation with a local about pigs, he realised now, must have looked altogether something else in the eyes of his lady love. This was especially true as the young woman was certainly attractive. However innocent these matters are in the minds of young men; they are rarely viewed with equanimity by their sweethearts. Simpson suspected that a spell in the doghouse would soon be his punishment. However, fate came to a strange rescue.

Just as Betty was about to give Simpson a piece of her mind and that piece of her mind was anger, one of the big labourers, who so resembled Dr Wilson and Raymond du Maurier, strode over and jerked back the shoulder of Simpson.

'I say,' said Betty, 'what's that lout doing?'

Simpson asked a similar question but in slightly more robust language. Moments later the labourer clouted him across the jaw. Simpson stumbled to the ground under the impact of the blow. The labourer pulled off his shirt to reveal an impressively made body. His intentions were clear. A crowd began to form and there were some shouts of support for the labourer who was called Timbo.

Betty was about to give Timbo a taste of his own medicine using Agatha's umbrella when she felt a restraining hand from Wilson who had arrived on the scene. He was about to intervene when Simpson bounced up from the ground and put his hand out to stop him. Seconds later he'd pulled off his coat and waistcoat and shirt to reveal an equally impressive torso, at least in Betty's highly objective view.

Timbo smiled and raised his fists, pointing them upwards. He was several inches taller than Simpson with a similar advantage in reach. However, his stance suggested he had no idea about how to box. Simpson, on the other hand, had honed his skill regularly against fellow cavalrymen. He began to circle the big labourer as the rest of the village descended on the latest piece of entertainment.

Children have an unerring instinct for these matters. Within seconds they had forced themselves to the front and began to chant, 'Fight, fight, fight.' This brought yet more people and a natural human ring was formed. Support was almost universally for the local man, so Betty had to shout all the louder to let Simpson know he was not alone.

Timbo made the first move, a wild loping right hand that started out from somewhere near Barnstaple. Simpson saw it coming and easily dodged it by moving inside and delivering a sharp jab to the nose of the labourer followed by a right cross to the solar plexus. That punch seemed not only to wind Timbo but half the spectators who groaned sympathetically.

Simpson moved backwards to avoid the swings that followed from Timbo. Another rapid one-two from the policeman bloodied the nose of the villager. Seconds later Timbo's eye was cut by a couple of swift jabs. This quietened the crowd as they realised that not only was the smaller visitor more than just a match for the big local, but he was also, technically, in a different league.

'Not so smug now are you Timbo,' said Simpson goading his opponent. The response was immediate, another wild swing which hit air followed by two short punches from Simpson to the labourer's kidneys that would have almost certainly fallen foul of the recently published Marquis of Queensbury rules for pugilism. Timbo fell to the ground in a manner that had one boy shout out, 'Timber.' This brought hoots of laughter from the villagers.

'Had enough?' said Simpson, aware that dispensing too bad a beating would not be well received by the locals. He watched Timbo rise groggily to his feet. Seconds later Simpson was on the ground himself courtesy of a blow from behind by the other labourer. A few of the villagers cried foul. Betty turned the air blue with her views on the subject earning admiring glances from Raymond du Maurier and Dr Wilson. Agatha was somewhat shocked by Betty's reaction although this was less to do with the fact that she had so publicly remonstrated with the culprit as much as her surprising knowledge of swear words.

Wilson once again looked to intervene. This time he was stopped by the fury that had turned Simpson's face into a mask. The policeman didn't so much rise from the ground as fly off like a tiger and in the space of seconds dished out a severe lesson to Timbo. When the big labourer collapsed to the ground bloodied, battered and bruised, Simpson turned his attention to the man who had hit him. It must be said the man was as big as Timbo, but his face had turned white. He tried to turn and evade Simpson but the crowd's desire for blood was at fever pitch. He was thrown into the ring.

One punch felled him, and he stayed on the ground without any obvious desire to re-engage battle. Simpson stood over him and waited for a few moments before waving it off as a bad job.

'You and your brother are a pair of absolute rotters,' snarled Simpson.

'He's not my brother,' said the labourer who was either blind or remarkably naïve about the subject of procreation beyond its physical accomplishment.

To the victor the spoils. In this case it was a rather prolonged kiss from Betty that brought cheers from the audience and no little cheer to the policeman. His eye had been cut by the sneak punch from the other labourer. Betty looked at it and realised that her man needed urgent medical attention.

'Come with me,' suggested Wilson and he led the victor away with Betty to attend to the eye.

Agatha meanwhile had caught the eye of Raymond du Maurier. He strolled over like a big cat in stalking prey.

'Impressive performance from your friend,' said du Maurier, puffing on a cheroot. 'If I'd known we'd have entertainment like that I might have tried to put a bet on.'

'Not very welcoming to visitors,' pointed out Agatha who was now feeling decidedly apprehensive following her exposure to such violence.

'Country ways are different,' said du Maurier, unabashed.

'Does that include cock fighting?' asked Agatha nodding towards the caged birds sitting on the other side of the green. 'I would say these ways are barbaric, sir.'

This made du Maurier's grin merely widen, much to Agatha's annoyance.

'I'm sure you can make a distinction between that and fox hunting or shooting. At least one of the birds has a chance in this case.'

'Interesting distinction,' said Agatha unsure of how to respond. She did not like being wrong-footed, especially by men. Her instinct was invariably to strike back. Harder. The jugular was her preferred target. There was something about the landowner she found unsettling. It seemed, however, du Maurier regretted what he'd said.

'How long are you staying Lady Agatha? You and your friends are more than welcome to visit my estate if you are free tomorrow.'

Agatha smiled and fixed her eyes on du Maurier.

'That is very kind of you, sir. However, we will return to London tomorrow. Our business, if it is to be conducted, must conclude tonight.'

Du Maurier nodded to Agatha.

'Yes, I suppose it must.'

They regarded one another for a moment. As du Maurier seemed uninterested in adding anything to his comment, Agatha filled the growing silence.

'It is somewhat out of my hands now. I cannot do anything more.'

Du Maurier smiled at Agatha and put a cheroot to his mouth. He bowed and walked away. Agatha watched him join Dr Wilson. The two men turned towards Agatha. Neither made any attempt to hide the fact that the conversation they were having was about her.

25

Ignatius Pollaky Narrative – 31st October 1876

I knew one thing with absolute certainty. I was in way over my head. Nearly fifteen years as a detective and I'd never felt this way before. The situation was desperate. I'd been threatened. My wife and family had been threatened. And I was no nearer finding the girl. And when I did, I had to pop some pills into her that would cure her of life. I'd had better weeks, trust me.

But that isn't the worst aspect of all this.

The thing keeping me awake at night wasn't just the threat. I'd been threatened before. It wasn't even the risk to my family, hell, I could shut myself in and fight it out with whoever came.

But who or what was I fighting? And worse than that, I really had no idea what to do about it. When you're bang out of ideas and fate is standing behind you drumming his fingers on the wall that's when it hits you worst.

I spent the train journey to Norwich either banging my head against the carriage window or crying. I don't know what the other passengers thought, well I do; they all left the carriage immediately.

My best bet was to follow Agatha. Why use my brain when I can use both of hers? It had worked before. It would again. The lives of my family were depending on it.

My thoughts turned to this Evelyn Carr kid. Someone had to be protecting her. Someone from the village or connected to it. I guessed Agatha would be thinking along similar lines. Between Agatha and me we'd figure out who.

Then...? My hand went instinctively to the revolver in my pocket. I felt like crying again.

There was no newspaper at the station when we arrived. This made me angry. I think it angered a few of the locals, too, when I let the world know what I thought of the backwardness of this Godforsaken place. Then I saw a rubbish bin. I damn near cheered when I saw what was in it.

The Times.

I had something to read, at last. And boy did I need to read it.

Did I ever tell you that I'm a master of disguise? Really. I, once, sat beside my wife in the park and she ignored me. She had no idea who I was. At least I think she'd no idea. You never know with women.

When I came off the train at Sheringham, I looked fifty years older. It wasn't just the disguise. Trust me, this case was having one hell of an effect on my nerves.

A horse was waiting for me at the station. Not my normal way of travel of late but I learned to rise a horse like a gypsy when I was a kid in Hungary. I'd missed it, I realised. I set off for the damn village, each yard closer increased the funk I was feeling.

I reached it after two hours. The festival was well underway already. The green was crowded, there were stalls dotted all over the place, kids screaming. Everyone was having a ball. Yet it still felt strange. The place was a reminder to me why I'd left Hungary and lived in London. I like people. But not this type of people. Inward, superstitious. I like to be around noise, and life. Particularly people who are cheating on their spouses. After this, I'll never complain again about standing outside a hotel on a wet Wednesday night.

Back in Hungary, every village had its own festival. I was used to this. It was all coming back to me as I watched the festivities. Maybe it was my mood, maybe it was the fear in my gut but there was an atmosphere about this place. Something dark. Violent. I could see some kid getting pelted in the stocks. There were caged birds at the other side of the green. It didn't take a detective to work out what entertainment the locals had planned there. Nice people. Attila the Hun would've loved it here.

Then I saw her. Lady Agatha Aston marching across the green like the British Army on manoeuvres.

In someone else's country.

26

Upper Outwell, Norfolk: 31ˢᵗ October 1876

Agatha stalked off in search of her friends. There was an undercurrent to this festival that was not to her liking. The sense of violence was palpable. This was no innocent village in the country. She wanted to be away from the place.

'Lady Agatha,' said a familiar voice.

Agatha turned around and found herself looking at Colonel Magilton. He was standing with the lawyer Joseph Parr and his wife, Amy.

'Colonel Magilton,' exclaimed Agatha in surprise. 'I don't know why but I wasn't expecting to find you here.'

'Why ever not?' laughed the Ulsterman.

'I didn't think you were from this area.'

'No more than you my lady,' grinned Magilton. This was a fair point and acknowledged by Agatha. 'I gather that you were in Bury St Edmunds recently.'

'Yes Colonel. The death of Phillip Larwood. It was quite a coincidence that you should also be the acting magistrate for this case,' replied Agatha.

'Indeed,' agreed Magilton. 'Although I would hasten to suggest it was more of a surprise your interest in the case than mine. May I ask what made you, Lady Elizabeth and Mr

Simpson wish to investigate the case? Do you believe it's connected to the death of Ophelia Carr?'

'Mr Simpson was asked to review the case. When we were there, we uncovered the fact that it bore similarities to a pair of cases twenty years ago.'

If Magilton was surprised by this then Parr was confused. He turned to Magilton with a frown.

'I say, what's all this Magilton?' asked Parr.

Magilton smiled and kept his eyes on Agatha, initially. Then he turned to Parr and Amy and said, 'Lady Agatha really is quite remarkable. If ever we needed proof that the police force of this country could be improved immeasurably at a stroke then we have it here, Parr. I mean it. Her ladyship is quite correct, Parr. There is a marked similarity between the death of Giles Shrimpton and Phillip Larwood.'

'I agree,' replied Agatha. 'Your verdict was correct in my view, Colonel Magilton. Perhaps one day we will know what happened to Mr Larwood.'

'You have your suspicions, though, Lady Agatha, I suspect.'

'As do you, Colonel Magilton.'

'And I have no earthly idea what you are talking about,' laughed Parr. Agatha shot a glance towards Parr. He was laughing. Nervously.

'I shall let the colonel tell you all. I must go and find my friends,' smiled Agatha taking her leave. She saw Nobby and Olivia speaking with Reverend Lumley. Rather than head to the house that Simpson and Betty had entered she walked over to them.

'Agatha,' exclaimed Nobby, 'What happened. I heard Simps was in a bit of a scuffle.'

'He was attacked, you mean, by those two brothers. It was an absolute disgrace. Thankfully he dealt with them both rather handily.'

'I'm glad to hear it,' said Nobby who seemed none too worried about what might have been an ugly incident. Olivia put a hand on Agatha's arm, however. There was a look of genuine sympathy on her face.

'It must have been upsetting, Agatha. I'm sorry you had to see it. I'm sorry for poor James, too. I'm glad he was able to deal with those two ruffians.'

The sense of shock at the sudden violence had begun to sink in with Agatha. She wanted nothing more than to be away now. However, part of her realised she should stay and see, at the very least, the bonfire being set off. She turned to Olivia but her attempt at hiding the upset she'd felt was unlikely to fool anyone.

'Thank you, Olivia, I shall be quite all right,' said Agatha, smiling unconvincingly. 'Do you know where Betty and James have gone.'

Olivia raised an eyebrow and smiled.

'I imagine she is nursing him back to full health. Shall we go and find them?'

'Good idea,' agreed Nobby.

The three went in search of Betty and Simpson. They'd entered a cottage not far away from where the fight had taken place. As Olivia had predicted, they found Betty providing ministrations that were unlikely to feature in many medical journals.

Agatha cleared her throat allowing a red-faced Betty to disengage herself from Simpson's embrace. The worthy policeman sported a smile as wide as The Wash and a bandage over his left eye.

'I'm happy to see you've made a swift recovery,' said Agatha archly.

'Betty has a wonderfully caring touch,' acknowledged Simpson with a grin.

'We noticed,' said Olivia laughing. 'I think Betty has taken to life in the county with great enthusiasm.'

'Along with Talleyrand,' said Agatha sotto voce. There was definitely something about the place.

*

As the sun began to go down behind the trees, the crowd assembled by the wooden frame that was meant to symbolise the Devil. It was bitterly cold now, but the rain had managed to hold off. Agatha was hopeful that once the bonfire started it might not only warm everyone up but signal the time for the party to leave. It had been a long day and a long evening lay ahead of them. Once more she felt apprehension slow her down. Each step towards the fire felt like she was wading through quicksand.

Raymond du Maurier was given the honour of lighting the bonfire. There were no speeches. He simply walked up to the wooden construction and threw a torch onto the straw at the bottom. A few children were also holding torches. They immediately threw theirs into the bottom of the bonfire. Within seconds Satan was once more, no doubt, feeling at home in the midst of flames.

A few of the villagers were carrying small musical instruments. Agatha could hear some lutes and accordions begin to play. Men, women and children immediately began to sing a song that resembled closely the entrancing melody that Agatha had heard earlier at the Punch and Judy show.

Young boys and girls as well as teenagers from the village held hands and surrounded the fire. As the music played, they began to dance. The dancers moved in a circle around the fire singing the haunting melody. Across the other side of the bonfire, Agatha could see Beatrix Dahlia and Ursula Piper's faces shimmering in the heat. They were standing with Raymond du Maurier. All were looking directly at her. Despite the heat of the bonfire, Agatha felt a chill in her bones.

The next half hour passed in a whirl. Agatha circled around the fire and met with the wives of Dr Wilson and Joseph Parr. Constable Tibbins asked her about progress on the case. She successfully avoided a second conversation with Colonel Magilton. Across the other side of the fire, she saw du Maurier. Their eyes met briefly.

Behind du Maurier she saw the young man that she'd mistaken for being a simpleton, Ned. He was on horseback and trotting around the edge of the green as if looking for someone. Agatha followed him as he rode slowly past the crowd. His eyes were like those of a hunter stalking his prey. He pulled his reins slightly and stopped to look at someone in the crowd. Agatha could not see who he was gazing at. She moved to her right but still could not see through the mass of bodies on the other side of the bonfire. She began to run to get a better view.

When she had run around to the other side Ned was gone. Her hands flopped limply by her side. Where had he gone? She felt an emptiness. Worse, her anxiety was increasing. She wanted to be alone. Away from here. Then, with a great effort she began to move again. She walked over to the other side of the fire.

And waited.

*

Agatha felt a tug on her sleeve. It was Olivia indicating that it was time to go. They looked at one another for a moment then Agatha took Olivia's arm and they walked towards the carriage. Somewhere in the background they could hear shrieks and men shouting. These were not the sounds of revelry. Something else had happened. Agatha smiled but did not look back. She didn't need to. Instead, she helped Olivia into the carriage before climbing in herself.

Betty arrived two minutes later. Betty's face was flushed as if she'd been running or was excited or, perhaps, a bit of both. She nodded to Agatha but said nothing. Nobby was the last to arrive. He popped his head into the carriage and checked to see who was there.

'Right. That's us, then.'

The carriage set off to the sound of music, singing near the fire and screams and shouts elsewhere.

'Most odd thing has happened,' said Nobby as the carriage set off. 'Someone let all of the cockerels loose. They're running amok now. Timbo and the others are having a devil of time trying to catch them.'

'How terrible,' said Agatha exchanging a glance with Betty who had a wry smile on her face. 'Who could have done such a thing?'

The carriage, on Nobby's instruction, turned back so that the occupants could have one last view of the bonfire. The flames were soaring skyward casting long shadows on the green. Agatha might have been impressed by the sight of the villagers dancing and singing in the night air, but her attention was focused on the comical scene behind the fire as men were falling over themselves trying to catch the birds.

The carriage slowed and then turned in a different direction. Slowly it started away from the village. As it moved towards the main path, Agatha's eyes caught sight of a young woman looking directly at her.

Long black hair hung down each side of her face. She was wearing a black shawl. Her face was pale which emphasised her dark eyes. A cold fear gripped Agatha and she felt her breathing become shallower and shallower.

'What's wrong?' asked Betty.

But Agatha's eyes were no longer fixed on the young woman. Instead, her focus had shifted to a dark figure standing twenty feet behind her. His features were blurred by the shimmering heat of the fire, but Agatha would have known him anywhere.

Ignatius Pollaky began to walk slowly towards the young woman.

James Simpson watched Timbo and his half-brother from behind a stall. They were by the caged birds drinking tankards of cider. If Agatha's suspicions were correct, they would probably want to temporarily leave guarding the caged fighting cocks when the singing started. As ever, she was correct. The sounds of music and celebration were proving too much of a lure. They abandoned the birds and went over towards the bonfire.

Simpson observed all this from the shadow of the Punch and Judy stall. The villagers were singing a beautiful melody. Children and young people encircled the fire holding hands. They began to move around the fire.

In the distance, Simpson could see Agatha running around the side of the fire, but he couldn't make out why she was doing so. She stopped and her arms hung by her sides in a resigned fashion. She returned a minute later to where she'd been standing. Then, unseen by Agatha, a woman dressed in black approached her from behind.

A hand grabbed Simpson by the shoulder. Simpson froze.

'James,' whispered Betty.

'I say,' said Simpson, turning round. 'That was jolly clever, I didn't hear you there. Scared me half to death.'

'Old trick I learned in school, come on, now's our chance. Have you seen?' whispered Betty in an urgent tone.

'Yes, they left a few seconds ago. Forward, march, what?'

Betty glanced at Simpson. One part of her wanted to berate him for treating this matter like some school yard jape. Another part of her wanted to kiss him for his obvious devil-may-care attitude. The bandage across his eye made him look awfully handsome, she thought.

Taking advantage of the fact that the two men were no longer guarding the caged birds, Betty and Simpson tracked round the outside of the green in the shadows. They reached the birds without being met by anyone.

'You keep look out Betty,' ordered Simpson.

So masterful, thought Betty.

Simpson proceeded to rip the cage doors off with his bare hands.

So strong, thought Betty.

The cage doors were bound by hemp, so the display of animalistic potency was perhaps wishful thinking on the part of the love-struck sleuth. Within seconds the cockerels exploded out of the cages. And started to fight one another.

'Oh,' said Betty in dismay.

'Oh,' said Simpson, equally disappointed. 'Can't be helped. Their nature, I suppose. Let's make our escape before someone sees us.

Betty was already on her way as the fighting had spilled out in her direction. She didn't want to become involved in the melee.

'Stupid birds,' whispered Betty. She and Simpson darted around the outside of the perimeter in the direction they'd come. They were a quarter of the way around the green when they heard the first shrieks to indicate that people were now aware that the birds had quite literally flown the coop.

'I think they've noticed,' said Simpson, laughing. He turned to Betty who was grinning from ear to ear. She's so full of adventure, thought Simpson. It was jolly exciting.

The Witchfinder General Murders

A dark figure stepped out of the shadows as they ran towards the other side of the bonfire. Neither stopped but Betty would have recognised him anywhere.

Ignatius Pollaky and Betty stared at one another for a moment and then Betty turned around and sped after Simpson. Pollaky looked back in the direction from which they'd come. A few of the men were chasing the birds and trying to catch them without much success. Had Pollaky been in a better mood he'd have enjoyed the spectacle. But he was on edge and stayed only momentarily. He walked down the gentle slope towards the bonfire.

Pollaky reached the edge of the green and surveyed the scene. The singing round the fire was interrupted briefly by the escaping birds but recommenced. A number of labourers were chasing the birds while other men, dressed like landed gentry, watched in amusement.

Agatha was talking with a woman dressed in black. She turned and her eyes met Pollaky's. Another, very striking woman, approached Agatha. She touched her arm and said a few words. Pollaky could see Agatha nodding and then the two ladies left the other woman.

Pollaky stood and watched as Agatha and the other woman entered a closed carriage at the edge of the green. Seconds later Betty arrived and climbed in, too. Another man joined them soon after. Within moments, the driver flicked his reins and the carriage set off. Pollaky followed the passage of the carriage as it did a sweep around the edge of the green before turning.

Just as it did so, Pollaky began to walk towards the woman Agatha had been speaking to. The carriage passed near to him and he briefly caught Agatha's eye before it disappeared into the night. The woman was also following the progress of the carriage. She held her black shawl tightly to protect against the cold night air.

'Pollaky,' said a voice from behind.

Pollaky turned around. It was Simpson.

The young detective nodded to Pollaky and then left to retrace his footsteps back around towards where he'd created havoc with the bird cages. One of the birds was peppering the ground nearby with its beak.

Simpson smiled down at the cockerel who stopped what it was doing and glanced up at his rescuer.

'There's a good fellow,' said Simpson, before walking on towards where the labourers were failing so spectacularly to catch the birds. By now children had joined in the chase and were adding further to the confusion of the scene. On the other side of the green, he caught sight of du Maurier and the two doctors, Wilson, enjoying the show. He set off towards them. When Simpson glanced back towards Pollaky, he could see that the Hungarian had disappeared.

Walking across the green proved more hazardous than Simpson had anticipated. He had to dodge several flying tackles from men trying to get hold of the escaped birds. One of them crashed down near the feet of Colonel Magilton and Joseph Parr.

'Aren't you going to lend a hand, colonel?' asked Simpson with a broad grin.

Magilton laughed along with Parr.

'This is the most diverting entertainment I've had in years,' laughed Magilton.

I must take you to the Madame Jo Jo's in Piccadilly sometime, thought Simpson. A couple of semi-dressed harlots pouring a goblet of wine down your throat might just conceivably top the sight of yokels falling over themselves chasing birds.

'I wonder what could have set them off?' asked Simpson innocently.

'One of the children, I'll be bound,' suggested Parr. 'What do you think, Magilton?'

'My very thought, too. I wouldn't be in that young pup's shoes if they ever find out who did it.'

Simpson chatted with the two men for another few minutes before moving over towards du Maurier and Dr Wilson. He was struck, once more, by the strong resemblance between the two men. It was clear that both men were also rather amused by the scene playing out before them. The big landowner fixed his eyes on Simpson.

'I don't suppose you saw what caused this?' asked du Maurier. The cheroot stayed firmly in his mouth.

Just at that moment Constable Tibbins appeared, out of uniform, breathless from having been part of the posse chasing the birds.

'It's no use, sir, these birds are impossible to catch.'

'Leave them, then,' ordered du Maurier. 'Half of them are fighting amongst themselves anyway.'

Tibbins left du Maurier to relay the orders. Activity ceased immediately and the labourers and villagers trooped dejectedly back towards the fire. Simpson watched them go trying not to smile too broadly. Very soon the singing and the dancing recommenced. On the half of the green vacated by the villagers, the birds were dotted around pecking the ground, fighting one another or standing on top of the stalls joining in heartily with the singing.

'Shall we join them?' asked Wilson.

'Good idea,' agreed du Maurier. He looked at Simpson and then glanced towards a group of horses tied to a wooden post. Returning his gaze to Simpson, there was an intensity that unnerved Simpson and he was a man not given to anxiety. There was fear, too, in the landowner's eyes. That much Simpson could read. And something else.

Rage.

Then du Maurier spoke. It was a more of a whispered snarl.

'The chestnut.'

28

He was standing less than six feet from her. Even he, Pollaky, could not miss. He'd never liked guns. Avoided them whenever he could. He fired one shot. The sound of it echoed through the night. They'd hear it in the village for sure.

There wasn't much time, however. Horses would come soon. Hooking his hands underneath her arms he dragged her towards the tree. She weighed next to nothing. Her body fitted easily into the shallow grave. He grabbed the shovel and threw the soil over the body until it was completely covered. He stood looking at the mound. Then he walked over to the small black colt and climbed up into the saddle. He looked up.

As he'd suspected someone was coming. Horses' hooves beat against the hard ground. A gentle kick and Pollaky's horse began to walk briskly away. He kicked again. The pace of the horse speeded up as it headed over the rise and away from the cottage. The sound of hooves in the distance grew louder. It was difficult to be sure, but it sounded like just one horse to Pollaky. He kept going, though.

His job was complete. He had to get home.

The last train to Norwich was at ten o'clock. There were two hours or more to travel. He could just about make it. Then he would take the first, morning train from Norwich to London. He'd be back at home by mid- morning.

Jack Murray

A full moon illuminated the cottage and the oak tree as a horse and rider raced up the hill. He pulled up near the oak tree and leapt off the horse. The horse snorted and gulped in the air.

The man looked around and then saw the mound on the other side of the oak. He stopped and put his hand to his mouth. He was trembling. From the shallow grave he could see a piece of dark cloth sticking out.

The dark shawl *she'd* been wearing.

The sound of a twig breaking stopped him just as he was about to walk towards the grave. He looked around and frowned. Then, a second noise. This time from above. He uttered an oath and looked around before glancing upwards.

Above him a dark crow sat on a branch and gazed down at him curiously. He picked up a twig and threw it at the bird. It missed by several feet. The crow did not move.

'Damn bird,' said the man and moved again towards the grave.

His eyes discerned the marks on the ground where the body had been dragged into the grave. He stopped to look then continued on his way. He was within ten feet of it when suddenly he saw the soil move. He stopped. It was definitely moving.

Then a body exploded out from the soil. It was a woman. A woman with wild grey hair and a face caked with mud. She was screaming.

At him.

'But you're dead,' said the man in a whisper.

She stopped screaming and pointed to him. In a low growling voice that seemed to come from the very bowels of hell she said one word.

'Murderer.'

'You're dead,' he repeated. 'How can this be?' Terror gripped him. In the distance he could hear the sound of hooves. It was like a stampede coming towards him. A lot of horsemen were on their way here. Panic descended on him like a plague. He felt inside his pocket.

His hand closed around a knife.

With his breath coming in grunts, he stumbled forward with the knife in his hand. He would end this once and for all. There was time. He could kill the old woman and dispense with the knife. In this darkness no one would find it. He could return tomorrow and hide it forever. In the space of those few seconds the panic that had gripped him evaporated.

He was thinking again.

He couldn't understand what had happened but there was still time to get control of the situation. He reached the old woman. She would not look up. Instead, she stared stonily ahead.

His arm went back as if to strike.

The bullet hit him in the shoulder. He fell backwards in agony. Footsteps. He turned his head which caused a wave of pain to course through his body.

'Who are you?'

Then his eyes focused, and he realised he was looking up at the young policeman Simpson. He watched as Simpson kicked away his knife. The same foot came to rest on his chest.

'Don't move,' said Simpson.

He heard another noise. The sound of a door opening. Other people were coming. Then he saw them. Those two interfering women, Lady Agatha and Lady Elizabeth. Then the Earl of Manningfield and that woman who pretended to be a witch, the countess.

But how was Ophelia Carr still alive?

Then he saw. The old woman rose from her grave and stood alongside Lady Agatha and Simpson. Only it wasn't an old woman. He'd been fooled. The hair had been streaked with chalk and mud.

It was *her.*

It was Evelyn Carr. Alive. Pollaky would pay. His family would pay. It was too late now. Events had been set in motion that even he could not stop.

*

'Release him, James,' said Agatha. As she said this the other horsemen arrived. There were shouts and then they came running. Agatha turned around and saw half a dozen men from the village.

Raymond du Maurier arrived at the scene. He went straight to Evelyn Carr. She fell into his arms sobbing. The landowner held onto her as if his life depended on it.

'My little girl,' he repeated over and over. 'You're safe now. You're safe.'

Agatha looked down at the man on the ground and said to Simpson.

'You can let Colonel Magilton get up. I think there are enough people here to deal with him.'

Magilton rose groggily to his feet, clutching his shoulder. His face was a mask of hatred.

The Witchfinder General Murders

'How did you know?' he snarled at Agatha. There was an enigmatic smile on her face. Magilton felt a strong hand grip his arm causing him to grimace in pain. He turned around and saw one of the labourers who so looked like du Maurier.

Simpson stepped back and let Magilton pass. Timbo looked at Simpson. They nodded to one another and then Timbo pushed the colonel towards a cart that had just arrived. Sitting alongside the driver was Constable Tibbins. The constable's face fell a little. This could have been his first big arrest. Instead, he was the last to arrive. And now would be the first to leave.

He was just the cab driver.

*

Agatha felt a hand on her arm. It was Olivia. She was in tears. What is it about a woman in tears that makes other women want to cry also? Within seconds, Agatha felt her eyes stinging. She and Olivia embraced.

'Thank you, Agatha. Nobby was right about you.'

Agatha smiled and replied, 'Thank you Olivia. If it hadn't been for you, we'd never have organised this...' Agatha looked around her.

'It was you Agatha,' said Olivia simply. She looked up as Nobby put his arm around her waist.

'You never change, old girl,' said Nobby. 'Still sharper than a...'

'Thorn?' offered Agatha with a smile.

Nobby laughed, 'You know what I mean.'

Betty, in the meantime, had been offering a rather idiosyncratic salutation to Simpson for his excellent marksmanship. When she came up for air, she took her man by the hand and led him over to Agatha.

'Another case closed,' announced Betty, happily.

211

'You'll soon be a Chief Inspector at this rate, James,' said Agatha. 'Good shot.'

'I couldn't miss,' said Simpson, modestly, 'even in this light.'

The group turned to walk in the direction of where the carriage had been deposited, some fifty yards on the other side of the hill.

As they walked, Agatha heard some footsteps from behind. It was du Maurier with Evelyn Carr.

'Thank you,' said du Maurier, simply. It was heartfelt. His arm was around the young woman and Agatha could see clearly, for the first time, how alike they were. Dr Wilson appeared moments later. Half-brother and half-sister thought Agatha. She laughed at the thought of them being sweethearts. Evidence first, conclusions after. This was a better approach which she knew she would forget immediately if they ever had another case.

Du Maurier held out his hand and Agatha shook it.

'I'm glad we've caught this terrible man,' said Agatha. She turned to Evelyn. 'There will have been more victims than just your mother. I'm sure of it. But you're safe now, I think.'

Agatha held her hand out to Evelyn. For a moment the young woman seemed to recoil. There was something in her face that Agatha could not understand. She shook Agatha's hand very briefly. Tears formed in her eyes and she tried to smile but could not.

'Is something wrong?' asked Agatha, alarmed that she'd done something wrong.

Evelyn Carr shook her head. Too quickly. Then she forced a smile which the tears gave lie to.

'I'll see you again,' said Evelyn then she turned away. Du Maurier looked confused and immediately followed his daughter. Dr Wilson stood with Agatha and the rest of the group.

'We'll see you at the carriage, Agatha,' said Betty, with one eyebrow raised.

Agatha watched them leave and then turned to Wilson. She laughed embarrassedly.

'I thought that you and Evelyn were sweethearts.'

Wilson laughed too. It was an attractive sound. She could happily listen to it for a long time.

'Not quite, as you can see.'

'Yes,' replied Agatha. 'I'm not sure if I can say anything else without appearing foolish.'

Wilson took her hand. It felt warm. Strong.

'You could never be foolish. You're an incredible woman, Lady Agatha. I wish you would stay longer with us.'

Oh, it was tempting. His voice. Those looks. But this was a strange, strange place. In truth, she was desperate to get away. This was not her world. It was somewhere alien. The culture, the values, the way of living all seemed not only from a different country but a different century. This would become a prison to her, she knew.

'I should join my friends,' replied Agatha. There was little regret in her voice.

Wilson took her hand and without shifting his eyes away from hers, he kissed her hand.

*

The journey back to Holbrigg Hall was a frustrating affair for Betty. Agatha seemed to be in one of her moods. Simpson was sitting on the other side of the carriage from her and the cab driver appeared to be intent on killing them all such was his haste to return to the Hall. All in all, it was a pretty poor show.

213

Betty folded her arms and stared out of the window. Somewhere in the distance she saw the fire lighting up the sky over Upper Outwell.

She was glad to be leaving.

Odd place.

29

9 Portsdown Road, London: 1ˢᵗ November 1876

The instruction had been quite clear. Unless he received a telegram saying 'STOP', then he was to continue. It suited him. The pay would pay double. Money for old rope. Just the wife, he said. The kids would bring too much down on them. Make it look like an accident. Pollaky wouldn't have a leg to stand on.

He waited until ten in the morning. Normally the telegrams came before nine. He rose from his seat, checked his pockets and headed out onto the street. Don't risk a cab, he'd said. Of course, it was raining. Bloody English weather.

He walked with his head down and ignored everyone on the street. Don't draw attention to yourself. At near six foot five this wasn't going to be easy. By the time he reached Portsdown Road he was fair soaked and in a bad mood. His mood worsened a second later when he bumped into a man coming around the corner of Portsdown Road. He was about to give him a piece of his mind and even a bunch of fives when he saw how tall he was. Almost as tall as him.

The other man smiled and said, 'Sorry, wasn't lookin' where I was going.'

'S'alright.'

He continued on his way. Rain was splashing off the pavement now. The trouser bottoms were wringing. The leather of his shoes sodden, and he could feel water underfoot. The first thing he'd buy with the cash was a pair of new shoes.

Water dripped down his face or maybe it was perspiration. The apprehension was growing. This wasn't his first time but even so, it wasn't easy. Number nine was up ahead. He turned and walked down the pathway. The portico supported by the white pillars offered some shelter.

He put a mask over his face. He looked like highway man. He rapped on the door. Hard. Then again. Through the frosted stained glass, he saw a small figure wearing black. Probably a maid.

The door opened.

If it was a maid then it was the ugliest, slyest piece of old baggage he'd ever seen. Such is the way with expectations. When your mind has told you what you're meant to see and it proves otherwise, it takes a little bit longer to process the discrepancy and act on the information.

It wasn't a woman at the door. It was a man. The man smiled up at him and said, 'Good morning.'

He reached into his pocket for the razor. It wasn't there. Strange. This was the last thing he'd checked before he'd left the house.

A voice from behind.

'Looking for this?'

He spun around. It was the man he'd bumped into a few minutes earlier. He was brandishing the razor in one hand.

'What the...'

The sentence went unfinished as the man's other hand crashed into his face. He collapsed to the ground semi-conscious.

'Well done, Lee,' said Sergeant Cartwright, taking the razor from Lee 'the Lifter' Lanniston.

'We're quits now, sarge?' asked the pickpocket hopefully.

'Yes, Lee. Stay out of trouble,' said Cartwright, knowing full well he wouldn't.

'Will do, sarge,' lied Lee in return. He gave the policeman a mock salute and walked away.

Cartwright looked down at the prone figure below. He gave him a surreptitious kick and then turned to find a young boy looking at him. He was around ten years of age.

'Who might you be?' asked Cartwright.

'Francis, sir. Is this the bad man who wanted to hurt us.'

A voice from upstairs shouted down. It was Mary Ann Pollaky. There was just a hint of fear in her voice.

'Francis, come up here immediately.'

Cartwright and the boy rolled their eyes in unison. Mothers the world over were the same. Well, perhaps not Cartwright's. She'd abandoned him long ago in favour of the bottle. Young Pollaky looked down at the man who was in a foetal position on the ground.

'Did you kick him?' asked the boy in a bright manner that suggested approval. There was just a hint of hope in his voice, too.

'I did,' admitted Cartwright.

The boy nodded and thought for a moment. Cartwright smiled inwardly.

'Can I?'

'Aye, go on son. Just don't tell your mother.'

Jack Murray

30

Grosvenor Square, London: 2nd November 1876

The arrival of James Simpson to Agatha's mansion proved to be a more restrained affair than Betty would have liked. When you are accompanied by the Chief Superintendent of the Detective Branch, it was always likely to put a dampener on the kind of welcome Betty had in mind. Instead, she had to content herself with a smile and a nod. She did pat his backside surreptitiously, however, as they walked into the drawing room for afternoon tea.

This was the first time that Betty had seen Simpson since they'd parted the previous morning. She was bound for London. Simpson stayed on to conduct a search of Colonel Magilton's house just outside Swaffham.

'You'll never believe what we found,' said Simpson, excitedly.

'Evidence of devil worship?' asked Agatha.

Simpson's face fell while the smile on Dolly Williamson's face widened. Betty though had had just about enough. She glared at Agatha crossly.

'I think, Agatha, just once in a while you might allow someone a chance to reveal their news without showing off how smart you are. If I came across a know-all fictional sleuth like you in a book, I would certainly think twice about buying the next one.'

The Chief Superintendent had the good grace to stop smiling at this point and merely fixed a twinkling eye on the suitably chastened Agatha.

'You are quite right, Betty. My apologies, Mr Simpson. Please continue.'

Simpson waited for a nod from his boss which was forthcoming. Even Dolly Williamson indicated for him to start.

'Magilton has a large country manor just outside Swaffham. Keeps some very fine horses, too, I might add. In fact...'

Betty touched his knee and Simpson quickly regained his focus.

'As I was saying, he has a large country estate, however, he lives alone. Never been married apparently. He has few staff and appears to be a man dedicated, in his retirement, to hunting and being a magistrate in that order. The latter occupation took him the length and breadth of Norfolk and, as we saw, northern parts of Suffolk. He was highly regarded, I gather.'

'Now, turning to the house itself, and as you correctly surmised, Lady Agatha, it is clear that Magilton was a follower of some rather esoteric, shall we say, faiths. He has an extensive library which contained many books on religions and beliefs from around the world. Of most relevance to us was the large room upstairs. A chapel, for wont of a better description, dedicated to something that definitely isn't Christian unless we've started worshipping goats.'

'Good lord,' said Betty. 'Goats?'

Even Agatha was taken aback by this.

'I think I'll return to the Reading Room and find out more about this. How very strange,' said Agatha.

Simpson's face darkened at this point and he glanced at Williamson. This time it was the Chief Inspector who spoke. He cleared his throat and said, 'Our investigations are only just beginning in this matter, but we've reason to believe that Magilton may have used this chapel for unspeakable practices. In fact, we think there are a number of unsolved murders in East Anglia that may be accounted for by what we, that is, Mr Simpson, uncovered in this house. I hope you won't mind if I do not speak of them. Not, I may say, to protect you. Even I find the matter distressing.'

Agatha and Betty looked at one another. The troubling nature of this case, which had never been far away from the surface for Agatha, was now becoming all too plain.

'Magilton,' continued Williamson, 'was a very dangerous man. We do not believe he was acting alone. Mr Simpson and a number of my detectives will be working now to find other members of this sect, or cult.'

'I am convinced Phillip Larwood was in league with Magilton,' said Agatha. 'That is why he was killed.'

Williamson looked at Agatha in surprise.

'You believe Larwood was murdered?'

Agatha paused for a moment and then spoke slowly as she tried to order her thoughts on the matter. The death of Larwood had troubled her for reasons that had nothing to do with frustration at not being able to prove who had done it. She *knew* who had done it.

'Larwood was...executed, Chief Superintendent. Executed without having gone through due process. I have no proof of this. I can scarcely tell you how it was done without appearing

221

foolish. Nor can I say who did it. It would not be fair to toss accusations willy-nilly without so much as a shred of evidence to support them.'

Williamson leaned forward and fixed his eyes on Agatha.

'I would still like to know what you think on the matter, Lady Agatha.'

Agatha exhaled and shifted her attention to the window. To look at the others while saying what she was about to say would have sealed her discomfort.

'Evelyn Carr was in the cottage the night her mother was killed by Magilton, Larwood and a third person. She did not see any of these men, however. She was in hiding. Her mother died to protect her...'

Agatha felt the tears well in her eyes. She ignored the pleas of Simpson and Williamson to stop, however. Ophelia Carr deserved that much.

'She signed a suicide note hoping that it might save her daughter but knowing she would die. Such courage...'

Her sense of anguish, which had been building up over the last two weeks rooted in the growing realisation of the sacrifice Ophelia Carr had made, broke like flood waters over dam. Agatha broke down and wept. It was a few minutes before she was able to collect herself sufficiently to continue.

'She died rather than divulge the whereabouts of her child. Magilton, Larwood and the other man searched the house but did not realise that there was a hiding place underneath the floorboards beneath Ophelia Carr's bed. At this point we move into territory that means we can probably never prove that Phillip Larwood was murdered.'

'Go on, Lady Agatha,' urged Williamson.

The Witchfinder General Murders

'I believe that Larwood must have left behind an item of clothing. Perhaps a glove or a handkerchief; something that could have been used to identify him to Evelyn Carr.'

'How would she have done this?'

Agatha turned to Williamson.

'This is the crux of the matter. You must suspend judgement, Chief Superintendent. I am led to believe that Evelyn Carr, like her mother, has a gift. She has the ability to have experiences and sight outside of her own body: astral projection to give it its name. These can be divined through touching people or objects. I know this seems fanciful, but I have no other explanation for how she was able to identify Larwood but could not do so with either Magilton or the other person unknown.'

Williamson nodded and then asked, 'How did you piece this together Lady Agatha?'

'Well,' laughed Agatha, 'if you remember, it started with the nightmare. A nightmare probably brought on by reading about the case while I was distracted.'

Betty shifted uncomfortably as Agatha's amused gaze fell on her.

'I don't know if you have ever been to this village Chief Superintendent, but it has an atmosphere. I had a sense of uneasiness from the moment I set foot in the place. But to answer your question I was immediately aware that everyone knew what had happened.'

'Really?' exclaimed Simpson.

Betty raised her eyebrows at Simpson who immediately hushed up. Williamson seemed more amused by his assistant's reaction. He'd long since accepted where the limitations lay with the young detective.

223

'Yes, the Earl and the Countess of Manningfield clearly knew where Evelyn was hiding. It only became apparent to me on the second visit why. And before you ask, Chief Superintendent, we are, once again, treading in rather unbelievable territory. I will summarise by saying that East Anglia is famously associated with witchcraft. I was given to understand that this has various manifestations. The Earl's family had clearly married people who practiced this belief. And the practitioners, if I can put it like that, were known to one another. They knew that Evelyn was the daughter of Raymond du Maurier and they, quite rightly guessed that she would seek protection with him. Her various disappearances were merely a young girl going to see her father.'

'I gather Mr du Maurier has a rather large family.' said Williamson, smiling.

'Very prolific,' agreed Agatha.

'Did the Earl and Countess know why Mrs Carr had been killed?'

'Everyone knew why she'd been killed, Chief Superintendent. This was one of the reasons my suspicions fell on Colonel Magilton.'

'But why was she killed? And why now?'

'This is a story that starts goes back to the English civil war. Witch finding reached its zenith during this period. In particular, in East Anglia. You will remember the name Matthew Hopkins, no doubt. He was not the first witchfinder, but he was the self-appointed Witchfinder General. The practice died out as the civil war ended. By then Hopkins had passed away. But that civil war was replaced by another. Where previously women and men had seen innocent people murdered for their beliefs, or more likely for money, they began to use their skills to exact revenge.'

'One of the women I spoke to suggested that the connection between witchcraft and devil-worship had always been misdirection on the part of the witchfinders. These people used it as justification to carry out the vilest of crimes that were either a part of their own evil nature or as a sacrifice for their abominable beliefs.'

'Magilton, Larwood and other men like them have been involved in other murders. This loathsome man, Magilton, used his position as a magistrate to advance his own despicable program. I believe one or both was involved in the murder of Helena Jadis twenty years ago. The suicide, a few days later, of Giles Shrimpton was, in fact, a reprisal for this murder. Shrimpton was probably in league with Magilton. And so, it went on. These men would find people they believed to be witches and would kill them. Not just witches, I might add.'

'You ask me why she was killed, and the only answer I can supply is that they were in love. They were men who have been rejected by women they loved. Jealousy and humiliation fuelled a hatred of women. What I am saying, Chief Superintendent, although I cannot prove it, is that these murders, in fact witch finding, is borne of love. Love spurned that turns to a dark hatred. They use devil worship as a spurious spiritual crutch to vindicate their actions. All women were a target, but witches in particular. They feared witches because they believed some of them had gifts which could reveal to the world who, or what, they really were.'

'In order to find such women, they used various means. One of those was the British Library. The day Ophelia Carr went with Beatrix Dahlia to the British Library sealed her fate.

It allowed evil to enter the village of Upper Outwell which had, over the years, become a haven for this community. A community, I might add, that had protection from two wealthy landowners, both of whom had married women who held these beliefs.'

'Hatred borne of love,' said Williamson, his eyes were directed out of the window as he tried to comprehend the idea. It was almost banal. Yet he'd seen it so often in his life. Crimes of passion, murders driven by jealousy and revenge. These murders were the active negation of love. They destroyed that which the murderer most valued.

The room fell silent for a few moments. There seemed nothing more to say about why the murder of Ophelia Carr had been committed. Williamson rose from his seat followed by Simpson, and the ladies accompanied them to the front door.

'How is Miss Carr?' asked Williamson at the door. 'Have you heard from the Earl or du Maurier?'

'Yes, the Earl sent us a letter which arrived this morning. She is with her father. Apparently when Ophelia fell pregnant eighteen years ago, she did not tell du Maurier. He was part of a rich family. I gather they opposed the match.'

'Instead, she left the village and made a life in the north. She married a man and bore the child of du Maurier. When her husband died a few years ago, she returned. There was no hiding who the true father of Evelyn was. The villagers could see immediately. Father and daughter were reconciled. I believe that the villagers conspired to create the story that Evelyn often ran away from home to protect her. Magilton did not believe this which leads me to suspect that he had recruited someone from the village to his abhorrent dogma.'

'Yes, Simpson has alerted me to your suspicions on this. We have circulated his description, but I must confess, unless he falls foul of the law, it will be the devil of a job to find him. However, we must leave you. Thank you, again, Lady Agatha, Lady Elizabeth for your help. I'm sure our paths will cross again,' said Williamson, glancing at Simpson and then back to Agatha and Betty.

Simpson was oblivious to the exchange, but Betty brightened up considerably.

'I hope so, too Chief Superintendent,' replied Agatha.

'We are to meet Pollaky now and take his statement. He can fill in some of the missing pieces in this rather Byzantine jigsaw. Good day, ladies,' said Williamson, touching his hat.

Agatha smiled and replied, 'Well for once, I think, Ignatius deserves much of the credit. I'm sure he'll be the first to say so.'

Ignatius Pollaky's Narrative – 2nd November 1876

Look, there ain't no one admires that lady more than me. And sure, there's been times when I took credit for things that rightly lay with her. But let me tell you, and in all modesty, I broke this case. Make no mistake, without me, Lady A would still be in that Godforsaken village fluttering her eyes at the local doctor.

Now, I'm not saying that I broke this case because of some extraordinary piece of deduction. I'll leave that for the penny dreadfuls. There may have been a bit of luck involved.

Bad luck.

To be more precise, *my* bad luck. And, yes, perhaps that dame should get some credit for shaking the tree, or to be more precise, getting me to shake the tree with the advertisement. It obviously had a response although even she, as smart as she is, could never have foreseen what would happen.

So, you want to know how *I* broke the case wide open. When that hood threatened me, I knew one thing with crystal-like clarity. I would never find that kid alone. I needed Lady A. Of course, I needed Lady A. But when you have some tough holding a knife over your head and telling you not to tell anyone, you have to get creative. And here's how I broke the case.

The second advertisement, the one Lady A did *not* ask me to write, contained a message for her. I changed the wording so that she would look to a second advertisement that I placed immediately below. It contained instructions to look at a third advertisement. I laid out the whole story to her in those.

Now, I'm not the world's most God-fearing man but I can tell you I prayed my butt off that night. And I'll hand it to the lady, the next day my advertisement ran again and immediately below it was one from Lady A. She'd received my message and understood. I coulda kissed that dame there and then. Of course, as a married man I wouldn't dream of doing that. Do you understand? She told me to go to that damn village on the 31st and that she would put an advertisement in *The Times* telling me what to do.

Of course, as I told you, I damn near missed finding a newspaper that day until I saw one thrown away. And there it was. The plan. She'd spread it put over three advertisements. It all looked so simple. She'd hired a horse for me at Sheringham. I was to take it to Upper Outwell. At some point in the evening Lady A would contact Evelyn Carr then leave. Someone somewhere would create a distraction. I was to use that moment to take the kid.

And kill her.

Well, it was to seem that way. Then I was to leave and return to the train station at Sheringham. Lady A would do the rest.

I have to say the plan worked like a dream. I saw Lady A talking to the kid. Then another dame came along and took her away. I saw Mr Simpson and Betty create an absolute riot when they released those caged birds. Nice touch by the way. I like their style. That was the cue for Ignatius Pollaky to take the helm.

I strolled over to the kid. She spun around on me. She's a heartbreaker, that one.

'Are you Mr Pollaky?' says she.

I said I was. I asked her if she was Evelyn Carr.

'I prefer to be called Eva,' says she. Her voice was low and real quiet, yet it seemed to cut through the air.

I went to shake her hand, but she seemed to recoil like I was a leper. She was embarrassed. Said it was better if we didn't. I heard she sees things. Maybe that's what happens. She goes through life and sees things about the people she comes into contact with.

She'd make a helluva detective. Forget Lady A. This kid would be unstoppable.

She went with me to my horse while the yokels were playing chase-the-bird. I wish I coulda stayed to watch. It was hysterical.

She went on the horse first, then me. The plan depended on us being seen. Lady A was convinced the killer of Ophelia Carr and the man threatening me were one and the same. Our little piece of theatre was to draw him and maybe his henchman out.

I was to take her up to the cottage and shoot her. Then drag her into a grave someone had dug near an oak tree. When we reached the place, I can tell you my heart was beating like I'd been chasing Spring-Heeled Jack across the rooftops. She was ice and not just because of the cold weather, either.

I waited until I thought I heard a horse coming. Then I aimed the gun away but not too far away from the kid and fired. Lady A said we had to make it look like she'd been shot. This was in case someone was already there. Someone, that is, who wasn't Mr Simpson. I fired the revolver and she collapsed to the ground like she'd been hit. I was convinced, I can tell you. She had a way of contorting her body. It was eerie.

By this point I just wanted to leave. Much as I would have liked to stick around for the unmasking, I had a train to catch. A family to return to. A family that was being guarded by the police.

I dragged her into the grave and left.

Epilogue

He saw her first. It was always thus.

She walked onto the green and no one noticed. She walked onto the green like she'd never been away. Like a princess. Across the ground she floated, and he could not draw his eyes away from her.

He wanted to talk to her. Make her understand. Then he looked down at himself. The stains from the cream pies were still evident. Then she turned around towards him like she'd sensed him. He wondered if she knew. Their eyes met. There was no hatred in her eyes.

She did not know.

He couldn't stop himself. He never could with her. He ran towards her. But she shook her head. He could see fear suddenly rise up in her eyes. She was afraid of him. It was the same look she'd given him when they'd kissed.

She knew him. She'd seen inside him and she was scared. From that day she'd never spoken to him again. Whenever he appeared near her, she would run. Her mother would shout at him. The old baggage. She'd learned her lesson all right. No more would she shout. Not so easy with your neck broken, is it?

He stopped. Gazed at her. Tried to make her understand that everything he'd done was for her. He wanted to show his love, but she wouldn't let him. Her mother wouldn't let him. Who was she to treat him this way? A desolate emptiness overcame him just before the hatred rose like lava from a volcano.

Witch.

She turned away from and continued to walk towards the bonfire. He watched her go and knew it was over. He looked around at the festivities. He could see the policeman and the two women. The net was drawing in. Once they had her, they would see what had happened.

He had to leave.

He left.

*

The money the colonel had given him was more than enough. So was the letter of introduction. It opened doors that would not have opened otherwise. He and Mr Larwood had always looked after him. It was a shame that they had to hide in the shadows. Society was intolerant. It wanted orthodoxy. It wanted church on Sunday; love thy neighbour; thou shalt not...thou shalt not.

I shall, he thought.

I shall do whatever I want. I will be free like the colonel.

Other men were not like this. They were in chains. Until they could satiate their hunger, quench their thirst, live every desire, they could never be free. What this world foolishly considered profane was sacred. The colonel had shown him this. No depravity should go unexperienced, no wish unfulfilled. To judge another man as evil was to have the wrong premise. Failure to define your own morality was evil. Sacrificing your integrity for someone else's convictions was the true depravity.

233

Jack Murray

Virtue came not from sacrifice but from independence, from strength and from following your own passion wherever they took you. One could no more condemn a man for following his passion even if it exploited others than blame the wind for blowing down a wooden house.

Life was a senseless accident for many. The colonel had shown him that it did not have to be this way. Instead, life could be transformed into something extraordinary and beautiful. One could live within the customs of society but act outside them.

But only in the darkness.

*

He gazed up at the imposing redbrick building. It was silhouetted menacingly against the dark slate-grey sky. He knew he would feel at home here. He looked at the sign on the wall. It read: Kings College Hospital.

'First day?' asked the elderly man at the gate.

'Yes,' he laughed. 'Is it so obvious?'

'After a while you see certain signs,' replied the elderly man. 'Now what's your name?'

He showed him the letter.

'Does the E stand for Edward?'

'Yes,' said the young man. 'But I've always been called Ned.'

'Well, young man,' said the old man, 'one day everyone will know you by a different name. You better get used to it, son.'

The old man smiled when he saw confusion descend on the young man. He loved to tease the new ones like this, but they always laughed in the end.

'What name would that be?' asked the young man, curious.

'You'll become Dr French one day.'

The young man smiled. He liked hearing the old man say it.

The Witchfinder General Murders

Dr French.

It was a few years away yet. His studies were only beginning. Soon, though, like the colonel, like Mr Larwood he would be an esteemed member of society. Looked up to by all. Valued for the service they provided. Free to do whatever he wanted. To live how he wished. A life without fear. A life without limits.

A life without conscience.

THE END

Please consider leaving a review. They are oxygen for independent writers like me!

Jack Murray

This is a work of fiction. However, it references real-life individuals. Gore Vidal, in his introduction to Lincoln, writes that placing history in fiction or fiction in history has been unfashionable since Tolstoy and that the result can be accused of being neither. He defends the practice, pointing out that writers from Aeschylus to Shakespeare to Tolstoy have done so with not inconsiderable success and merit.

I have mentioned a number of key real-life individuals and events in this novel. My intention, in the following section, is to explain a little more about their connection to this period and this story.

For further reading on this period and the specific topics within this work of fiction I would recommend the following: The Witchfinder General, Ronald Bassett, Paddington Pollaky: Private Detective by Bryan Kesselman, Plain Clothes and Sleuths by Stephen Wade; the documentaries and podcasts of Ronald Hutton.

This book wears its influences on its sleeve. Agatha Christie, of course, but The Witchfinder General, both the book and the film was an influence as was 'the Wicker man and the original book, Ritual by David Pinner.

Matthew Hopkins (1620 – 1647)

The most famous English witchfinder from this period. Hopkins' career started during the English Civil War. Nominally with the roundheads he may have used this alternative career as a way of avoiding service. The actual office of Witchfinder General was never bestowed by Parliament and was very much his own creation. His activities took place mainly in East Anglia.

His career began in 1644 and lasted until his retirement in 1647. He and his associates are believed to have been responsible for hanging over 100 people for activities associated with witchcraft. In this he was aided and abetted not only by associates such as John

Stearne but also local Puritan administrators who appeared to take the law into their hands and apply viciously. He was paid 20 shillings per town for his 'services'.

His book 'The Discovery of Witches' outlines the methods by which he proved evidenced his cases. Their targets were the mentally ill and the old. The accusations were often based on reprisals, gossip and jealousy. The Witchcraft Act was repealed in 1736.

Adolphus 'Dolly' Williamson (1859 – 1920)
Williamson was a Scotsman and the first head of the Detective Branch of the Metropolitan Police. Following a restructure in 1877, caused by a corruption scandal, the Criminal Investigation Department (CID) was formed with Williamson as the first head.

Williamson joined the force in 1850 and was a sergeant to Whicher during the period around the Road Hill House Murder. Williamson was a quiet, middle-aged man who walked leisurely along Whitehall balancing a hat that was a little too large for him loosely on his head' according to Major Arthur Griffith. He was known as 'the philosopher for his abstract and intellectual manner.

Ignatius 'Paddington' Pollaky (1828 – 1918)
Pollaky was born in Hungary but came to live in Britain in 1850. He became one of the first and best-known professional private detectives in Britain. He also worked with London's Metropolitan Police, instigating alien registration in Britain. Apart from his detective work, he was the London correspondent for the International Criminal Police Gazette for more than 25 years.

Nathaniel Druscovich (1841 – 1881)
Son of a Moldavian immigrant, the rise and fall of Nathaniel Druscovich is almost worth its own series of books. He joined the Metropolitan police after spending time in Europe. He was a sergeant by the age of 22, an inspector by the age of 27 and a year later he was Chief Inspector. Many of his cases were high profile and he also,

because of his facility with languages, worked on international cases. By the age of 35 he was in jail for fraud and dead at 39.

About the Author

Jack Murray lives just outside London with his family. Born in Ireland he has spent most of his adult life in the England. His first novel, 'The Affair of the Christmas Card Killer' has been a global success. Five further Kit Aston novels have followed: 'The Chess Board Murders', 'The Phantom' and 'The Frisco Falcon' and 'The Medium Murders' is the fifth in the Kit Aston series. The next Kit Aston will be released in late 2021.

The Agatha Aston mysteries is based on the very popular character Aunt Agatha from the Kit Aston mysteries. These are set in a period during the mid-1870's.

There are two more series to mention. The first has just started. It features the grandson of Chief Inspector Jellicoe who features in the Kit Aston mysteries. The mysteries are set in 1959.

In 2022 a new WW2 trilogy will be released through Lume Books. This all features characters from the world of Kit Aston.

239

Jack Murray

EXCLUSIVE!

A TASTER FROM THE UPCOMING KIT ASTON NOVEL -
THE BLUEBEARD CLUB.

*This exclusive snapshot of the novel features Agatha Aston in
1921. In this scene, Agatha and Mary Cavendish have been invited by
Alfred Hitchcock, whom they met in an earlier Kit Aston novel, to
take part in a motion picture that he is involved with.*

Mary and Agatha sat side by side in front of a large mirror lit by
small bulbs. The younger of the two ladies was enjoying the
experience immensely. It would be fair to say Agatha, less so.
However, this was Mary's last week of freedom. Not that the life
ahead of her was one of serfdom either but she seemed quite
enthused by the idea so Agatha had felt duty bound to go along with
her.

'Not too much makeup young lady for me,' ordered Agatha to
the young lady whose job, it seemed was to cake faces with brown
clay. 'and this young lady hardly requires any.'

'The lights require a certain amount of makeup otherwise you'll
look like a ghost, Aunt Agatha.'

'As I understand it, our appearance will be fleeting at best and I
suspect that the both the men and the women in the audience will be
looking at you.'

Mary turned to Agatha and giggled affectionately. Agatha shook
her grumpily although, in truth, she was rather looking forward to
the whole thing. But she had a reputation to maintain.

'Lady Mary, will you come with me to the changing room,' asked
the young woman who had been applying the makeup.

'Oh,' said Mary. 'Am I not just wearing this?'

'No, Mr Hitchcock had something else in mind. I also need to fit
the blonde wig. You'll be standing in for Miss Glynne, you see.'

It was Agatha's turn to laugh now. This surprised Mary which
only made Agatha laugh even more. There was more than 'I-told-
you-so' in Agatha's merriment. Even Mary couldn't resist a smile
when she'd left the room.

The Witchfinder General Murders

The blonde wig turned out to be the least of Mary's surprises. Her costume was, if anything, an even greater source of wonder.

'It's her nightdress,' explained the young woman. She left the changing room to allow Mary to don what there was of her costume. Mary appeared a few minutes later.

'Are you sure?' she asked uncertainly.

'Mr Hitchcock was most insistent.'

Mary was given a dressing gown and led onto the set. Awaiting her was Agatha who was sitting with a cup of tea. Mary O'Connor, the screenwriter of the film, was nowhere to be seen but Alfred was busily directing the crew on placement of props while the cameraman fixed a film spool onto the camera. Mary joined Agatha and waited for a few minutes while the crew made ready to begin shooting the scene.

Finally, all seemed ready and Alfred strolled over to the two ladies. There hadn't been much to say to the technicians. Rather, he'd wanted to extend the amount of time he could surreptitiously look at the blonde, bewigged Mary. His forehead was beaded with sweat and a lake had formed under his arms. This was not entirely due to the heat of the lights.

'Thank you once more, I cannot tell you how grateful I am for this. Now, let me tell you about your scene.'

Mary and Agatha both leaned forward. The two ladies were, by now, fully engaged in the film-making process and had agreed that a trip to see a motion picture would need to be made before they took the train to Little Gloston the next day.

'Lady Mary, as you know you are filling in for Miss Glynne. She plays the young woman Joan Farrant who is now remarried with someone she loves. Lady Agatha, you will play her mother. This part is being played by Minna Grey. You, Lady Agatha, will come into the room and break the news to Lady Mary, or Joan, that her first husband is still alive.'

The two ladies nodded. This seemed straightforward enough.

'How should I react, Alfred?' asked Mary.

'In motion pictures, we rely on a more physical reaction,' replied Alfred. 'I believe Mr Powell prefers a hand perhaps covering the mouth.' Alfred proceeded to demonstrate this particular trope. Then he walked over to the bed. 'Perhaps we could rehearse the scene a little. Lady Mary, if you could remove your dressing gown and step into the bed.' Alfred's voice seemed a little tight at this point.

'Does Lady Agatha wake me?'

'No, you shall wake yourself. The room will be in darkness. We shall see you step out of the bed and go to the French windows. You will throw open the curtains. At this point, Lady Agatha will knock in the door. You say, "Who is it?". Then Lady Agatha enters the room and breaks the news. Lady Agatha, we will film you saying, "Eli is still alive", to Lady Mary.'

'Certainly direct,' commented Agatha huffily.

Alfred's smiled enigmatically and he replied, 'Your character is very strong-willed and not a little volatile.'

'That will really stretch you, Aunt Agatha,' said Mary, a grin on her face.

Agatha raised an eyebrow and said sardonically, 'Yes, dealing with a young romantic fool of a daughter will require much imagination on my part.'

Mary climbed into the bed and waited for the instruction from Alfred.

'And action,' said Alfred from his, or rather Paul Powell's, director's chair.

Mary rolled a few times in the bed and then threw the bedclothes away. She rose up and padded over to the French windows, yawned daintily and then pulled the curtains aside. She didn't have to act being blinded by the light. The lights behind the windows were the brightest she'd ever seen. Moments later, there was a knock and the Agatha entered from behind a rather flimsy set door and said her line.

Alfred ended the rehearsal by saying, 'And cut' although no actual filming had taken place. In truth he'd barely been able to speak such was the loveliness of the vision that he beheld. There really was something about blue-eyed, blonde, ladies that made him feel something indefinable, or all too definable if he thought about it sufficiently.

Alfred requested several more rehearsals before shooting commenced. By now he was not only satisfied that Mary had the scene under control, he'd all but melted into the chair. And not just him. Several of the older technicians were palpitating badly. The scene was finally completed to Alfred and, it must be said, the crew's satisfaction a few minutes later.

Mary and Agatha had both enjoyed their acting stint. Each had played major parts in school plays over the years and the smell of the greasepaint never truly leaves you. Mary donned her dressing gown and walked over to Alfred with Agatha.

'Well that was fun,' said Mary brightly.

Alfred couldn't have agreed more. He was too overcome with something that might have passed for emotion to do anything else but nod.

'Tell me, Alfred,' asked Agatha. 'Won't the audience see that it is a different actress playing the young woman?'

'From this distance I doubt they would notice,' replied Alfred. Agatha glanced over at the brightly lit French window. She had a strong suspicion that the brightness of the light flooding through the window and the flimsiness of Mary's nightdress might have combined in a way that had proved agreeable to Alfred. Well, it was too late to do anything about it now.

'Ahh,' said Agatha nodding. 'It all makes sense now. Will that be all then?'

'Yes Lady Agatha, Lady Mary. I cannot begin to tell you how grateful I am for your help today. I'm so glad you enjoyed yourselves.'

Alfred's smiled unctuously.

'We did,' said Mary.

'Yes,' said Agatha before adding as an afterthought, 'Almost as much as you and your colleagues.' She fixed her eyes on Alfred for a moment and then swept off towards the dressing rooms followed by a mystified Mary.

The Bluebeard Club will be published in late 2021.

Jack Murray

Acknowledgements

It is not possible to write a book on your own. There are contributions from so many people either directly or indirectly over many years. Listing them all would be an impossible task.

Special mention therefore should be made to my wife and family who have been patient and put up with my occasional grumpiness when working on this project.

My brother, Edward, helped in proofing and made supportive comments that helped me tremendously. I have been very lucky to receive badly needed editing from Kathy Lance who has helped tighten up some of the grammatical issues that, frankly, plagued my earlier books. She has been a Godsend!

My late father and mother both loved books. They encouraged a love of reading in me. In particular, they liked detective books, so I must tip my hat to the two greatest writers of this genre, Sir Arthur and Dame Agatha.

Following writing, comes the business of marketing. My thanks to Mark Hodgson and Sophia Kyriacou for their advice on this important area. Additionally, a shout out to the wonderful folk on 20Booksto50k.

Finally, my thanks to the teachers who taught and nurtured a love of writing.

Printed in Great Britain
by Amazon

19831762R00150